Praise for the Raine Stockton Dog Mystery Series

"An exciting, original and suspense-laden whodunit... A simply fabulous mystery starring a likeable, dedicated heroine..."
--*Midwest Book Review*

"A delightful protagonist...a well-crafted mystery."
--*Romantic Times*

"There can't be too many golden retrievers in mystery fiction for my taste."
--*Deadly Pleasures*

" An intriguing heroine, a twisty tale, a riveting finale, and a golden retriever to die for. [This book] will delight mystery fans and enchant dog lovers."
---*Carolyn Hart*

"Has everything--wonderful characters, surprising twists, great dialogue. Donna Ball knows dogs, knows the Smoky Mountains, and knows how to write a page turner. I loved it."
--*Beverly Connor*

"Very entertaining... combines a likeable heroine and a fascinating mystery... a story of suspense with humor and tenderness."

--*Carlene Thompson*

DOUBLE DOG DARE

A Raine Stockton Dog Mystery Book #8

By Donna Ball

Published by Blue Merle Publishing

Drawer H
Mountain City, Georgia 30562
www.bluemerlepublishing.com
ISBN 13: 978-0-9857748-4-4
ISBN 10: 0985774843
First printing December 2013

This is a work of fiction. All places, characters, events and organizations mentioned in this book are either the product of the author's imagination, or used fictitiously.

Cover art by www.bigstock.com

CHAPTER ONE

The sound of exploding china was like a gunshot. My two Australian shepherds, Mischief and Magic, darted under the kitchen table and even Cisco dropped his waving golden tail, laid his ears flat against his head, and made himself as small as it was possible for a seventy-two- pound golden retriever to do while still remaining upright and poised to run. Usually, as he knew very well, sounds like that were followed by yelling, and the yelling was usually directed at him, usually with good cause. This time, however, I simply stared in astonishment at the shattered remains of my Golden Retriever of America Club mug that were scattered across the floor. I hadn't dropped it. I had thrown it. One minute it was in my hand, ready to be filled with my morning coffee, and the next minute I had smashed it on the floor. I couldn't believe it.

Maude had given me that mug for Christmas over ten years ago.

My name is Raine Stockton. I am the owner and operator of Dog Daze Boarding and Training, and up until a few weeks ago, Maude, who had been like a mother to me for most of my life, had been my partner. Generally speaking, I am as calm and collected as anyone you'd ever want to meet; you have to be when you work with dogs. I hardly ever throw things, or drop them either. I don't know what happened. One minute I was looking at the cup, the next I was smashing it on the floor. I guess I'd been under a little stress lately.

"Wow," I said. I was unable, for a moment, to drag my eyes from the mess.

Miles watched me from his seat at the table, his own coffee cup paused midway to his lips. "To say the least," he agreed mildly. His expression was unruffled. Or at least I hope it was unruffled, and not the kind of look you give a person you are trying to keep calm while you leave the room to make a call to the mental hospital. Come to think of it, I had been getting that look a lot lately, and not just from Miles.

We had been seriously seeing each other for less than a year, but Miles was slowly moving his way up the relationship ladder toward semi-Significant Other, despite the fact that we had absolutely nothing in common and in almost every meaningful way were polar opposites. He traveled the world; I rarely left the mountains of North Carolina. He hobnobbed with the society elite; I went to pot-luck dinners. I was a dedicated conservationist, and he made his rather impressive living by destroying natural beauty and putting up condos. Though I frequently accused him of not understanding me at all, I sometimes secretly suspected he knew me a little too well. This was one of those times.

I cleared my throat in embarrassment and went to the broom closet, pausing along the way to snatch a handful of dog treats from the cookie jar. I quickly swept up the mess, and as soon as the floor was safe for dog paws, I called my guys over and apologized, plying them with treats and neck rubs. No one forgives and forgets faster than a dog, especially when there are treats involved, and in a matter of moments I was awash in wriggling fur and happy doggie breath, laughing as I dodged wet kisses and tried to keep myself from being knocked over by the melee. You have to try really hard to stay upset when you're around dogs, and frankly, at this hour of the morning, I didn't have the energy.

Miles said, "Do you have an up-to-date passport?"

The question surprised me as much as my dropping and/or throwing of the mug must have surprised him. Both came out of nowhere, and neither had a rational explanation. I said, standing up, "Of course I do."

My father had been a district court judge in the small North Carolina mountain town of Hansonville where I still lived. He had also, as I had only recently found out, been a lying cheater, just like my ex-husband, who had abused his office and disgraced everything he had ever stood for and taught me to believe in, but that's beside the point. The point is that before I went off to college, he and my mother, who had no idea he was cheating on her and lying to us both, had taken me to Raleigh to apply for my first passport. My mother made me promise to keep it up to date, telling me that it was a symbol of the world that was about to open up before me. She had died only a few years later, and in memory of her I had always kept my passport up to date, despite the fact that I had only used it twice: once when my ex and I had gone on our first honeymoon, camping in Canada, and again when we had gone on our second honeymoon, fishing in Mexico. I'm sure my mother had hoped the passport would be used for more exotic destinations, and come to think of it, so had I. But hey, we all face disappointments in life.

Some bigger than others.

I had started to get another cup of coffee but, feeling the scowl pulling between my eyebrows, I wasn't sure I trusted myself with the china. I veered away and opened the door for the dogs. "Come on, guys," I invited. "Run play."

The two Aussies raced out into the misty summer morning, but Cisco, who rarely left a room when there was still food on the table, elected to stay.

"How'd you like a few days at the beach?" Miles said.

"I'd like it fine," I said, keeping my voice bright and airy with a determined effort. "But you don't need a passport for that."

"You do if the beach is in the French West Indies."

I gave a short bark of laughter that I hoped didn't sound as mirthless as I felt. "Oh, yeah, like I can just drop everything and sail half- way around the world with you."

I made my way over to the table where a plate of bagels that Miles had brought all the way from Atlanta was waiting, along with cream cheese, smoked salmon, soft butter and my Aunt Mart's unbeatable strawberry jam. I forgot that Cisco was under my feet—how, I can't imagine, since he's almost *always* under my feet—and spoke sharply when I almost tripped over him. "Cisco, for heaven's sake, will you *move*?" I pointed angrily to the dog bed on the other side of the kitchen. "Place! Now!"

Cisco's ears went down, Miles's eyebrows went up, and I felt like a cad as Cisco slunk away and dropped down onto his bed with a sigh, head between his paws. In fact, I felt like crying. I felt like that a lot lately, too.

Miles got up from the table and went to top off his coffee. "One," he said, "we're not sailing, we're flying. Two…" He filled a second cup and handed it to me. "It's not half-way around the world. It's just St. Bart's. Practically Florida. Mel gets out of school for the summer on Friday and I promised her the trip if she got an A in earth science on her last report card. I figured we'd leave Saturday morning."

Now he had my attention. Melanie was Miles's ten-year-old daughter, and he sometimes accused me of liking her more than I liked him. Sometimes he was right. Since both Miles and Melanie lived full time in Atlanta a good three hours away, I rarely got to spend enough time with her during the school year. Miles had a place in St. Bart's and he had been promising to take me there for months, but every time we made plans to go something always came up. A lot of people might have considered a trip to a romantic place like St. Bart's with a man like Miles to be irresistible in and of itself, but what put it over the top for me was that fact that Melanie would be coming along. For a moment I actually considered it. But only for a moment.

I said, "You don't think you might be going a little overboard? When I was a kid I got ice cream for getting A's."

Miles had had full custody of Melanie for less than a year and he was still feeling his way around some of the finer points of fatherhood. I knew he did not appreciate unsolicited advice on parenting— which was probably why, on this occasion, I chose to give it—and he usually let me know. This morning he clearly had another agenda.

"Yeah, well, I got a quarter. Melanie gets a trip to the Caribbean. What do you say?"

I gave a swift sharp shake of my head. "Don't be ridiculous. I can't just take off like that. I've got three dogs. Just what am I supposed to do with them?"

He pulled out a chair for me at the breakfast table, shrugging one shoulder. "Bring them with you. As long as their health certificates are up to date, there should be no problem."

I was outraged. "Put my dogs in the cargo hold of an airplane? In the middle of the summer? Are you crazy? Do you know how many dogs suffocate or die of heat stroke or get lost in airports or—"

He held up a hand for peace and spoke over me. "No cargo hold," he promised, "no airports, no heat stroke. We'll take a private plane, four hours in the air max. The dogs will fly first class, just like the rest of us."

Did I mention I'm dating a rich guy? There are certain advantages. "Four hours in the air with three dogs," I muttered grumpily as I took my seat. "Sounds like the perfect vacation to me."

Of course, now I was just being difficult, although anyone who has ever taken even one dog on vacation with them will have to admit that it's not the most relaxing way to spend a holiday. But the truth was that I really did want to go, as impractical as the whole idea was, and now I resented Miles for putting the possibility in my head.

"Suit yourself." Miles sat across from me and reached for a bagel. "But Melanie will pout the whole time if you don't bring Cisco. Not to mention what Cisco will do."

I frowned, absently spooning strawberry jam on my onion bagel. Miles watched me, but said nothing.

"Cisco's not going to do anything," I said, and the dog in question lifted his head hopefully at the sound of his name. "He's going to be right here with me. You might be able to hop on your private plane and go jetting off to the islands whenever the mood strikes, but I have a business to run. I'm teaching three obedience classes and two agility classes a week, not to mention our therapy dog visits on Saturday, and I'm trial secretary for the agility trial next month *plus* I'm on the committee for the Midsummer Night's Dog Festival for the animal shelter, and—"

"I thought you said your classes finished up this week."

"Well, they do." I plopped a thin slice of smoked salmon atop the jam. "But I start another set in two weeks, and I have registrations to send out and confirmations to e-mail and bookkeeping to do—"

"And didn't you spend all last week on the entries for that agility trial? Didn't you say something about being finished with it until next month?"

Sometimes I loved Miles for remembering the little details of my life like that. Other times... not so much. You'd think a man who ran two corporations and who-knows-how-many subsidiary companies would have better things to do than to remember every little thing I said.

I took out my frustration on the salt shaker, shaking it vigorously over the salmon on my bagel. "For heaven's sake," I told Miles tersely, "I run a boarding kennel. I can't just take off whenever I want to. What am I supposed to do, close it down?"

"Why not?" he replied, buttering his bagel. "That's what sole proprietorships do, you know, when they can't be on site—they cease operations for a limited period of time. How long since you did that, Raine? When was the last time you had a vacation?"

I concentrated on spreading a big glop of cream cheese atop the salted salmon strawberry bagel. Vacation? For the past ten years, my vacations had been weekend dog shows, workshops or training conferences, and those were possible only when Maude was available to take my place. Of course, Maude wasn't here anymore. No more vacations for me.

"I can't afford to close down," I muttered. But I did not look at him when I said it because he knew perfectly well that I could... for a few days, at least. He had been here when I had come into an unexpected windfall over Christmas, enough to completely remodel the kennel building, buy all new equipment, and put quite a bit away for a rainy day. Or a vacation.

"Five days," he said. "A week at most. Sunshine, surf, clear blue waters, plenty of tropical drinks with those little umbrellas in them... you'll be a new woman."

I bristled at that. "What's wrong with the old one?"

But Miles, as I should know by now, was not that easily baited. He replied, "Are you sure you want me to answer that?" And he bit into his bagel.

I plopped another spoonful of jam atop my bagel, scowling at him. "Thank you very much for starting out my day on such a cheery note. As if I didn't have enough to deal with, now I get to think about how I'm *not* at the beach while I'm scooping up dog poop and hosing down kennels. Well, have fun."

"My point exactly," Miles said. Sometimes he reminds me of a jungle panther, lying in wait for the first verbal misstep and then pouncing on it to make his point. "You're doing the job of two people and you're working yourself to a frazzle. And let's face it, Raine, you've still got issues over all that business with your father and Maude that you haven't dealt with, and until you do things are only going to get worse. Maybe some time away will help you sort things through."

So there you have it. My father, whom I had idolized all of my life, had had an affair with

Maude, my mother's best friend and my closest confidant, the one person in the world I trusted as much as I did myself, and lied about it both to my mother and to me for twenty years. In the end the lie had almost gotten me killed. The average person might have a few issues with that, but I was not average. Oh, sure, I had been upset at first, but I was over it. The worst part was that, knowing what I knew— and with Maude *knowing* that I knew— we both agreed it would be impossible for us to work together any longer. As soon as the last paper was signed dissolving our partnership, Maude retired to Florida and left me to manage on my own. And I was managing just fine. What was done was done.

I had been about to take a bite out of my bagel, but I put it down deliberately. I went very still, very calm. "Thank you, Dr. Young, for that piercing analysis. You can always be counted on to get straight to the heart of the matter. Where did you get your psychiatric degree again?" And because I knew he would have a comeback that was a lot wittier than mine, I went on without giving him a chance to reply. "For your information, I don't have any issues. It's over, done with, and in the past. I'm fine. Everything is just fine, or at least it would be if you'd stop pestering me about going on vacation and let me get to work. Honestly, you're the most self-centered person I know. You think the whole world revolves around you and I'm supposed to just drop everything whenever you're in the mood to play. I have a life, you know. Why don't you think of someone besides yourself for a change?"

"You're yelling at your boyfriend because he offered to take you on an all-expenses-paid vacation to a luxurious island resort," he pointed out, sipping his coffee. "But you don't have issues. Oh no, you're doing just fine."

I snatched up my bagel, took a bite, and almost choked.

One corner of Miles's lips curved up slightly; otherwise his expression was deadpan. "Maybe a little ketchup?" he suggested.

Somehow I managed to swallow the disgusting mix, and washed away the taste with a gulp of coffee. Cisco, who was watching me like a hawk, had no trouble picking up on the slight curve of my index finger that beckoned him over, and he was on his feet like a shot, nails scrabbling on the tile floor. He sat beautifully by my chair, big brown eyes bright and expectant, ears lifted, tail swishing on the floor. I scraped off the over-salted cream cheese, peeled off the salmon, and gave it to him. Onion bagels were not on his diet. Cisco swallowed the morsel faster than he could taste it and waited hopefully for more, tail swishing faster. I said, "Sorry, big guy. That's it."

I glanced at Miles, somewhat chastened, and added, "I'm sorry to you, too. I'm sorry for yelling, I'm sorry I can't go to the beach. Thank you for offering."

He glanced at his watch. "Gotta go, hon." He finished off his coffee and stood. "Some of us have to work for a living, you know."

Miles, who required almost no sleep, often drove up from Atlanta for the day to oversee the progress on the ridiculously over-priced and outrageously over-developed fly-in golf community he had desecrated half my mountain to build. That was how he had happened to arrive at my door at dawn with fresh bagels, and since it was a weekday, I knew he would be driving back in time to greet Melanie when she got home from school. I did not want us to part on bad terms.

I persisted, "It was nice of you, really. I appreciate it. Are you mad at me?"

"Of course not." He dropped a kiss on my rumpled hair. "I'll send a car for you Saturday morning."

"What? What for? I told you, I'm not going!"

He scratched Cisco under the chin and turned to the door. "Six a.m. sharp."

I twisted in my chair to follow his movement. "I'm not going!"

"Love you, babe." He winked and added, "Talk to her, Cisco."

"I'm serious. I'm not— "

But I was talking to the closed door.

And that was, more or less, how I ended up five days later sitting in a butter-soft white leather seat on a private plane with a golden retriever panting in my ear, gazing out the window at an ocean so clear and so blue that the only word for it is Caribbean. Vacation. What a concept. Island vacation? Not in my vocabulary.

I had not capitulated to Miles. I was not stressed. I was not overworked. I did not have issues. I was fine. But it seemed that everyone I knew had ganged up on me over the past week, conspiring to make certain I did not miss this opportunity. My friend Sonny, who was building an animal sanctuary of sorts on her property outside of town, had invited Mischief and Magic to stay with her while I was gone. My part-time kennel help worked overtime in hopes that, if he got caught up on all his chores, I would change my mind and go. My clients offered to rearrange their schedules. My Aunt Mart even volunteered to move into my house to look after both the dogs and the kennel. The very thought of my elegant Aunt Mart slogging through the mud in work boots to exercise dogs and sanitize kennel runs every morning brought a blush of shame and horror to my face. Was I that desperate? That pathetic? That obviously in need of being taken care of?

Apparently.

In the end, though, it was the phone call from Melanie that did it. Melanie reminds me a lot of myself when I was her age—wild, untameable black curls, big ugly glasses, a little overweight, and completely obsessed with dogs. Of course she's a lot smarter than I was at age ten— or even now, I sometimes think—and is certainly more well-traveled.

Her eight month-old golden retriever, Pepper, was recovering from spay surgery and, while cleared to fly, was strongly advised by the vet against climbing, running, romping on the beach, or swimming, and that was what she had called about. "Dad says we should leave her with the pet sitter," Melanie reported glumly. "He's probably right. But what's the point of going if I can't take her? Maybe I should just stay home. At least I'd get to be with Pepper."

I knew how much Miles valued these rare getaways with his daughter, and I knew how disappointed he'd be if she bailed. On the other hand, there was nothing worse for a well- meaning parent than a disgruntled kid who'd rather be anywhere but with them; I knew because I had been that disgruntled kid more than once.

And I knew how to fix it.

I said sympathetically, "That's tough. But Pepper's stayed with the pet sitter before and you said she had a great time."

"Yeah, but…"

"And I was kind of counting on you to keep Cisco company at the beach. You know, while I'm catching some rays."

"Really?" Her voice lit up like sunshine. "You're coming? You're bringing Cisco? You better believe it! Say, I've been reading about how Homeland Security trains bomb-sniffing dogs. If we could find some accelerant and some fuses, I'll bet we could train Cisco in no time!"

Cisco was a certified search and rescue dog, a therapy dog, a Canine Good Citizen, and an agility champion—all hard won accomplishments that had taken years to achieve. But Melanie had ambitions in dog training way beyond my own, or Cisco's. And accelerants were out of the question.

I suggested, "Or we could just let him play Frisbee on the beach. After all, it's his vacation too."

She thought about that for half a second, then agreed cheerfully, "Sure! I can't wait to show him the town. Do you know they let dogs in restaurants there? It's French!"

And so it was settled. The Aussies moved in with Sonny for the duration, I closed the kennel for a week, and the next thing I knew I was loading Cisco, his crate, his bed, his toys, his dog food, his backpack, his leashes and his grooming supplies—along with my meager suitcase filled with shorts, sundresses and swimsuits—onto a private plane at a small airport midway between Atlanta and Asheville. Melanie could hardly contain her excitement. Miles was looking very self- satisfied. I began to wonder if I had been manipulated. And by the time our plane circled the small landing strip on the tropical island of St. Bart's, I didn't care.

I secured Cisco in his crate at the back of the plane for safety's sake on landing, and when I returned to my seat the co-pilot was chatting with Miles and Melanie about landing procedures. Miles's eyes were twinkling as he fastened his seat belt and told me, "You're about to see why most people prefer to fly into St. Martin and take the ferry over."

I saw what he meant when I looked out the window and saw the plane lining up to approach the world's shortest runway. I gasped and closed my eyes when the wheels touched the ground, convinced we were going to end up in the ocean, but before I could even wonder whether the plane carried life vests for dogs among its emergency equipment, we had come to a complete, if rather abrupt stop.

"That was cool!" declared Melanie, eyes big as she wrestled out of her seat belt and climbed over her father's feet to the aisle. "I'll get Cisco."

"That was not cool," I told Miles, my heart still pounding as I unfastened my own seatbelt. "I thought the point was to get away from stress."

"Starting now," he promised with a wink. He grabbed my hand as I plopped my sun hat on my head and we made our way toward the exit.

CHAPTER TWO

There was very little activity at the small air strip, although most of it did seem to involve Rolls Royces, Land Rovers and limousines with blacked out windows, and far fewer people than I might have expected—which I assumed was a by-product of the death-defying runway. Ours was the only plane at the airport and we were the only passengers, so it took a matter of moments to get our passports stamped and Cisco's travel documents checked. By the time Melanie had taken Cisco on a bathroom break, our luggage was loaded into the waiting car, leaving me with barely enough to time to absorb the delicious tropical breeze and brilliant aquas and greens of the island before the driver was opening the back door of the car for me. "Welcome, mademoiselle, to paradise." He spoke with a slight French accent and had an affable sparkle in his eyes. He turned to Melanie, "And young mademoiselle, and…" Cisco, never one to ignore an open door, bounded into the back seat in front of Melanie. Our driver was completely unruffled. "*Monsieur la chien.*"

"That means dog," Melanie informed me, in case I didn't know, and climbed in after him.

I have to admit, up until this point I had been practically bursting with pride in Cisco. True, he's pretty unflappable in most situations, but he had never been on a plane before — although he had ridden in a helicopter and discovered it was not his favorite thing to do—much less a private plane with leather seats that cost more than my sofa and a buffet of croissants, muffins and cheeses that was left fully accessible throughout the flight, along with the fine china in which they were served, and a frost-white carpet with a gold logo emblazoned in it. Clearly whoever had designed the interior had not intended it to accommodate dogs. But he hadn't torn one seat with his claws, or knocked over one dish with his tail, or stolen a single croissant. And the way he bounded into the back of the limousine and took his seat just like any celebrity on Rodeo Drive made me wonder why I had ever been nervous about how he would do on the trip.

Pride, as they say, goes before a fall, and fall is what I almost did when, just as I was ducking to get into the car, Cisco's ears suddenly went forward, his muzzled swiveled, and before I could stop him he barreled past me and across the parking lot, trailing his leash behind.

"Hey!" Melanie exclaimed.

I cried, "Cisco!"and lunged after him. Out of the corner of my eye I saw Miles, who had been consulting with the driver about our route, look around and put out a hand to stop Melanie, who was climbing out of the car after us. He was too late. Melanie and I raced across the parking lot in an almost-single-file with Cisco in the lead, hot on the trail of a large white sea bird that swooped far too close to the ground for a dog who had been bred to retrieve birds.

Running is Cisco's best thing; that's how he became an agility champion. I couldn't keep up with him on an obstacle course, and I had no illusion of catching him in an open parking lot. What I *did* hope to do was to keep him in sight until I was close enough to make myself heard over the low roar of engines and equipment that were the background noise of the small airport. He was maybe twenty feet ahead of me when we came around the corner of the compact terminal building and into another section of the parking lot.

Immediately I saw the car that was waiting at the curb with its engine in gear while a woman in a big hat, dark sunglasses and a long chiffon scarf obscuring her face hurried from the shadows on the building and into the back seat of the car. She was in such a hurry that something fluttered from her pocket as she ducked into the car and she didn't even stop to pick it up. The car started to move before she had completely closed the door. And Cisco was racing straight toward its path.

At moments like this, a kind of supernatural calm comes over me and everything Maude had ever taught me about dog training becomes a simple matter of instinct. Dogs respond to panic with panic, she had always said. They respond to calm with attention. I stood stock still, extending an arm to stop Melanie as she drew up beside me, and I called with loud, firm authority, "Cisco, halt!"

He stopped dead. Before he could change his mind I shouted, "Down!"

He dropped to the ground a few feet behind the car just as it pulled away from the curb at a high rate of speed—a lot higher, if you ask me, than was safe in a parking lot. As far as I could tell, the driver never saw any of us.

Okay, so we had practiced that particular maneuver every day of Cisco's life, and he'd performed it perfectly, under a variety of circumstances, ninety percent of the time. Still, I couldn't help thinking about that other ten percent, and wondering whether this time might have been one of them had not the bird long since flown out of sight by the time I gave the command. And I didn't completely relax until Melanie, trotting ahead of me, had Cisco's leash in hand.

Melanie was a good dog trainer, and she waited until I reached them, praised Cisco calmly for his quick response to my command, and released him before she took a dog biscuit from her pocket and tossed it to him, ruffling his ears while he gulped it down and then grinned happily at her, wanting more. It may seem counterintuitive to reward a dog who has just bolted across a parking lot and almost gotten run over, but one look at Cisco's panting face and happily wriggling body confirmed that he had no memory whatsoever of any wrongdoing, so what good would it do to yell at him about it? Dogs have a remarkable way of only remembering the things that have brought them the most recent joy. If only people could do the same.

I reached down and picked up the paper the woman had dropped just as Miles jogged up. "Everything okay?" he asked. He wasn't even winded, but he hadn't just chased a golden retriever at top speed across the parking lot.

"We're working on impulse control," I muttered, embarrassed.

"Say, Dad, guess who we just saw?" Melanie said excitedly. "Beyonce!"

I looked at her, surprised, and Miles said, "Is that right?"

She reconsidered. "Maybe it was Taylor Swift. She had a scarf over her face."

"Could have been J.K. Rowling," Miles suggested.

Her eyes lit up. "Hey! Yeah!"

"Celebrity watching," he explained to me. "It's one of our favorite things to do here on the island. What have you got there?"

I showed him the slip of paper I'd picked up. "J.K. dropped her boarding pass," I said. "She was in such a hurry she didn't even notice."

He glanced at it. "Or care. That's a ferry ticket, and it's been cancelled. She was probably throwing it away."

I looked back at it curiously and discovered he was right. The ticket was for the 10:30 a.m. ferry from St. Martin, and it had already been used. "Huh. I wonder why she was at the airport if she came over on the ferry."

"Who knows why famous people do anything? Come on." He dropped an arm around my shoulders. "We'll stop in town for lunch. There's a place I know that has the best pizza this side of Italy."

"And they allow dogs!" exclaimed Melanie. "Come on, Cisco, let's race!"

The two of them took off at top speed before either Miles or I could object, which was probably just as well. We were on vacation, after all.

The driver, who Miles explained was part of the concierge service he used whenever he was here, took us through the island shopping district where some of the most exclusive designers in the world had shops. I did not think I'd be doing any shopping on this street while I was here, but Melanie had a good time pretending to spot celebrities. I was surprised by the way the luxury villas—hundreds of them, it seemed— crowded the lush green hillsides in staggered layers, their tile roofs glittering in the sun, all of them vying for the best view of what had to be the most spectacular array of beaches and bays I had ever seen. The tranquil aqua waters were brilliant with the white prows of luxury yachts and sailboats, and I have to admit I twisted my neck once or twice to get a better view of the beautiful people sunning themselves on the gleaming teak decks of some of those yachts.

"We'll take the boat out to the Pain du Sucre islet before we leave for some snorkeling," Miles said. "I like to dive there when I get a chance. It's like nothing you've ever seen, absolutely gorgeous."

Snorkeling sounded like fun, but diving would have been better. I wondered if there was time to get certified while I was here.

Melanie echoed my thoughts. "Say, Dad, didn't you say I could start diving lessons this year?"

"I seem to recall saying something like that. Of course, that's bound to cut into your time playing on the beach with Cisco."

Miles winked at me while Melanie considered the trade-off, and I smiled back. Given the choice, I'm not sure what I would have decided either.

"Pardon, monsieur, if you'll permit me..." The driver glanced at us in the mirror. "If you will let me know the day you plan to dive in the Pain de Sucre area, we will be pleased to check availability for you. Unfortunately, the authorities have closed off access to certain areas while they complete their investigation."

I said, "Investigation?" and Miles leaned forward toward the driver's seat.

"What happened?" he asked. "I haven't heard about any storms since I was here last. Is there some environmental concern about the reef?"

"No sir, nothing of that nature. There was, I'm sad to say, a tragic diving accident yesterday and the matter is still under investigation. I am surprised this has not yet been reported on the American news."

Miles said, "Stupid people go diving every day and get themselves into trouble. Why would it have been on the news?"

"Pardon, monsieur, what I meant to say was that the victim was the American television actress Rachelle Denison. Sadly, she did not survive."

Miles sat back, looking disturbed, and murmured, "I'm sorry to hear that."

I have to admit I had never heard of her, but a questioning glance at Melanie, our resident television expert, saw her frowning with concentration. "You mean Helen from *Wolftown*? The werewolf queen," she explained to me. "You know, werewolves— they're like vampires only meaner." I admitted I did not know much about werewolves, and she went on, "Anyway, the show was about this pack of werewolves living in the suburbs and Helen was their queen… I don't think it's on anymore. Wow, too bad she's dead. She was pretty."

Miles said, "Is her husband here?"

"*Oui*, monsieur. It is my understanding they were diving together when the accident occurred."

Miles frowned. "That's rough." He explained to me, "Alex Barry. I know him. We're neighbors here on the island. I should stop by, I suppose."

I said, "Did you know his wife?"

"I may have met her once. I don't think they'd been married long. I haven't even seen Alex in years. We're not usually here at the same time. What a shame."

I placed my hand over his, and he let the melancholy fade. He smiled at me, clearly unwilling to let our vacation get off to such a maudlin start, and threaded his fingers through mine. "I'm sure they'll get it all resolved soon," he said. "But the snorkeling is great anywhere you go around the island. We'll make a day of it, maybe sail over to St. Martin if you're in the mood."

I liked the sound of that. Imagine, being able to do whatever you wanted, just because you were in the mood. I felt a grin tug at my lips that was as big as Cisco's.

Melanie said, "Say, Dad, are there sharks in this ocean?"

"There are sharks in every ocean, honey."

"Do you think the lady might have gotten eaten by a shark?"

"Let's hope not."

"Yeah, gross." She was thoughtful for a moment. "Maybe I'll wait until next time to start the scuba lessons. After all, we have company." She draped a companionable arm around Cisco's shoulders and he obligingly licked her face.

Miles winked at her. "Good call, Champ."

We stopped at an outdoor café where I had the best caramelized onion and goat cheese pizza I had ever tasted—which I later learned was probably due to the shaved truffles on top—and Cisco had grilled salmon, hold the lemon butter. I'm not at all sure what Melanie had, and she probably wasn't either, because, with the possible exception of the three and a half seconds it took Cisco to gulp down his salmon, she spent the entire time trying to distract him from his fascination with a yappy little bichon two tables down. It was good dog-training experience for her.

It was exciting, being this far from home, but also a little unsettling. The sky was so blue it hurt my eyes, even with the sunglasses, and I kept looking around for the mountains. Without them I felt exposed. The air smelled different and the sun was hotter. The voices around me spoke in half a dozen different accents, and none of them were familiar to me. But what struck me the most was how different the people were —svelte, sophisticated, beautifully groomed and perfectly put together, but for all that they were in what was arguably one of the most beautiful places in the world enjoying an exquisite gourmet meal with companions they presumably liked, none of them seemed particularly happy. I, on the other hand, am I lot like a golden retriever in that respect: when I'm having a good time, people know it. When I'm not, people know it.

My golden retriever role model had finally given up on the bichon—or perhaps had succumbed to the excitement of the trip and the soporific heat— and was stretched out under the table on his back, letting me rub his furry belly with my bare foot. "You know," I observed to Miles, "I'm really very provincial." That might have been considered stating the obvious, given the circumstances, but I was okay with that.

"So you are," Miles agreed. "One of the things I like best about you."

I didn't know whether to be insulted or flattered. It was Melanie who pointed out, "I don't think that's a compliment, Dad."

"Of course it is. I'm provincial too."

Melanie grinned at him around the straw of her virgin pina colada and inquired, "Am I?"

He pretended to think about it. "No. You're more sophisticated than either one of us. One of the things I like best about you."

Melanie giggled.

I liked seeing Miles in such a playful mood, and I could tell Melanie was enjoying his attention. I was starting to think this trip had not been such a bad idea after all. I sipped my own drink—also a virgin pina colada, which seemed to be made with ice cream and was actually better without the rum. "What I meant was," I explained to Miles, "I don't get out of the mountains nearly enough. It's a pretty big culture shock. So why did you end up buying a place here?" I glanced around. "This doesn't really seem like your kind of crowd."

Not, I realized suddenly, that I had any real idea what his kind of crowd was. Until now, we had only been together in my world—dog shows, mountain hikes, small town fairs—and he had always been comfortable there. But what if this strange and shiny place with its sleek, bored-looking people was where he really belonged?

But he reassured me in the next moment with a shrug. "I got the property in foreclosure. I'll sell it in five years for three times what I paid, meanwhile it more than pays for its upkeep in the rent I get from rich tourists. And the sailing is great."

That reminded me of what I had meant to ask him earlier. "Miles, I'm curious."

"Another one of the things I like best about you." Behind his sunglasses, I could almost see his eyes twinkle, and Melanie giggled again.

I went on, "Is it customary to close down an entire section of the ocean when there's a diving accident? Seems pretty impractical to me."

"It is impractical, most of the time. But I suppose it depends on the circumstances. If the site is unsafe, for example."

"But the driver didn't say anything about that. He just said the authorities were investigating. I wonder what they're investigating. Or do you think it's just routine? Maybe it's local policy to close the site after an accident."

Maybe I didn't mention that, in addition to my father being a judge, my uncle had been the sheriff of my small town for almost thirty years, a position my ex-husband now held. I had grown up around law enforcement, and thinking like a policeman had become a habit.

"Don't ask me, sugar. I'm just a provincial boy from South Carolina, and I'm on vacation. Anybody up for dessert, or are you ready for some beach time?"

"Beach!" both Melanie and I chorused, and Cisco, sensing new excitement, got up so quickly he bumped his head on the table. He shook it off, ready for anything, and as soon as I found my shoes, so was I. I could still take a lesson from my golden retriever, and, after all, I was on vacation too.

The car wound its way up the side of a hill, through a set of wrought iron gates that opened automatically to admit us, and down a palm lined shell drive to a long, sprawling stucco villa surrounded by deep, marble floored lanais and sheltered by a red tile roof. A sweep of green lawn arced away from the entrance on either side, and a trellis draped in brilliant pink bougainvillea led the way to an expansive patio at the side of the house, where I got a glimpse of a shimmering pool.

I looked at Miles accusingly. "You said it was a condo!"

"I do have a condo," he said, "but that side of the island is so crowded this time of year. The villa is much nicer."

Melanie wrinkled her nose. "And sometimes the ladies take their tops off on the beaches over there. It's gross."

"Gross," agreed Miles with a perfectly straight face.

"So you have two houses on St. Bart's," I clarified cautiously.

"No, I have a condo and a villa. The villa doesn't have a hot tub, but it does have a pool. I hope you're not disappointed." He pushed up his sunglasses so I could see the smile in his eyes.

I said, pretending to frown, "I'll let you know."

The car glided to a stop at the porticoed front entrance and Melanie pushed open the door almost in the same instant, practically tumbling out in her excitement. "Wait till you see the pool!" she said. "It's majorly cool!"

I grabbed for Cisco's leash and missed as he bounded out behind her and the two of them raced across the lawn. "It's okay," Miles assured me. "Everything is fenced and gated. Just don't give him the security code."

I got out and took it all in—the rugged green hills behind us dotted with red-roofed villas, the turquoise sea spreading out below the velvet lawn, the shushing sound of the ocean, the breeze that tugged at my skirt and my hair. I felt whatever was left of the tension of the past few weeks melt into the place where sea met sky.

Miles put an arm around my shoulders. "Gorgeous, isn't it?" he said. "This is what I wanted you to see. And this..." he turned me in his arms, pulling me close, "is what I wanted you to feel."

I draped my arms around his neck and leaned in for his kiss, but it was not to be. I heard a splash, followed by Melanie's delighted squeal of "*Cisco!*" and I winced, turning toward the sound. "Is he allowed in the pool?"

Miles gave a resigned laugh and followed as I trotted toward the pool area.

It was, as Melanie had promised, spectacular. The crystal blue rectangle was positioned in the center of a giant expanse of weathered teak, its infinity edge disappearing into the horizon at the exact point the ocean met the sky. I couldn't help wondering how that must appear to the golden retriever who was so happily paddling across the surface of the water now just as though he had every intention of swimming out to sea. The deck was lined with ten or fifteen luxurious chaises upholstered in bright yellow with turquoise pillows, and underneath a shady gazebo there was a dining area with a circular banquette upholstered in turquoise with bright yellow cushions. I could picture myself sitting here, gazing out over the ocean and sipping something cool and tangy, for the entire week in perfect contentment. The golden retriever swimming in the pool was optional.

I went over to the steps and called Cisco out. Melanie said, "We should have gotten him some pool toys while we were in town. Hey! I saw a dog paddling a surf board on You-Tube once. I bet we could teach Cisco to do that."

"As long as you teach him in the pool. He's not ready to catch the big waves yet."

Cisco felt the steps under his paws and Melanie leaned forward to grab his collar as he climbed out. Of course, the minute he was on dry ground he shook water everywhere, soaking Melanie and grinning when she squealed. Everybody loves a dog with a sense of humor.

I was faster to back away than she was and only got a few water splotches on my skirt, but I could tell it was going to be a long week unless we figured out some way to keep Cisco out of the pool. And I had only brought one quick-dry dog towel.

Miles said, "Run get some towels from the bath house, Mel, and dry him off before you come in the house." He touched my shoulder lightly. "I'll show you your room. And, " he added over his shoulder as we turned toward the house, "no going to the beach without an adult."

"I know, I know," she replied, wiping her wet glasses on the hem of her shirt, which only made them wetter.

"And Cisco is not an adult," I felt compelled to add, and she giggled.

The entire back wall of the house was made of glass doors, which were now open to the sea breeze and a sleek steel-and-granite kitchen that could have been lifted from the pages of a magazine. There was a marble-floored-living room encased in the same drop-dead views of ocean and sky as we had seen outside, furnished with low white leather sofas and tangerine accents. The bedrooms were up a single flight of open teak stairs enclosed by cable wire and flooded with light and blue sky from the tall windows that surrounded it.

"There are five bedrooms up here," Miles said, "and a nanny's room downstairs. Mel is down the hall, and here you are."

He opened the door to a large airy room with buttercup yellow walls and polished mahogany floors. In the center of the room was a tall four-poster bed dressed in a French provincial yellow and red floral comforter with red pillow shams and a bright red cotton throw arranged in a perfect triangle over one corner of the bed. A table held a vase of fresh flowers and a crystal dish of chocolates. Next to my bed there was an ice bucket containing individual bottles of mineral water and a bottle of champagne; there were wine glasses and a plate of fresh fruit on the night stand. At the foot of the bed was a Cisco-sized dog bed upholstered in the same pattern as the comforter, with a bright red dog blanket artfully arranged across one corner. And next to it was a silver dog dish embossed with raised bones, with a matching dish filled with water, a few ice cubes still floating on top.

I couldn't help laughing out loud with delight. "Miles, this is unbelievable!"

"Do you like it?" he asked, pleased. "I thought you would."

"Are you kidding me? Champagne, chocolate…a custom dog bed!" I went from one surface to the other, touching each one, as happy as a puppy in a dog park. "Silver dog dishes!"

"They're probably plate," he admitted. "The concierge service fixed it all up for you when I told them there would be a dog. They went all out for Pepper, too, when we brought her down last winter."

I went out onto the deck, inhaled the sea view, and waved down to Melanie, who was vigorously rubbing Cisco down with a towel on the pool deck below. "Be sure to dry his feet," I called, "or he'll track wet paw prints all over the floors."

Melanie waved back in acknowledgement and Cisco did his funny little three-legged dance while she started drying his paws one at a time.

"They're marble," Miles reminded me. "They can take it." He nodded his head toward another set of open doors a few feet away. "That's my room, by the way."

"Oh," I said innocently. "We share a balcony. How nice."

"And convenient," he pointed out. "In case you should, you know, need anything during the night."

"Oh, I'm sure I won't," I replied, deadpan. "I mean…" I turned back to the room and spread my arms. "You've thought of everything. What could I possibly need?"

He caught my hand. "Come on, you haven't even seen the best part."

"I thought this was the best part," I teased him, indicating the adjoining rooms.

He stopped and cupped his hands around my neck, looking into my eyes, touching his forehead to mine. "No," he said. "The best part is seeing you here, laughing, not worrying about dogs or competitions or training classes or other people's problems. Not getting shot at or threatened or stranded on a mountaintop or nearly blown up or run over by a truck on your own front porch. The best part is being normal for a change."

I forced an uncomfortable laugh. "If this is normal for you we have even less in common than I thought." But he was right. My life did tend to be filled with drama, and not all of it was of my own making.

I resolved, right then and there, to try to be more normal. At least for a week.

He kissed my nose and stepped away. "The best part," he reminded me. He swung open a door and gestured me inside.

I looked around at the pleasant tiled walls and porcelain fixtures. "A bathroom? I hate to disappoint you, but I've seen them before."

Without a word, he extended his arm toward what appeared to be the shower cubby. I stepped inside and into a lush tropical garden with the sky for a roof and cedar plank walls. Bromeliads bloomed from moss baskets that hung from the walls, and a veil of trailing vines dotted with tiny fragrant white flowers hid the shelves that held soap, sponges and shampoo.

"It's a Balinese outdoor shower," Miles explained. "This side of the house is built into the hill, so all the bedrooms have them. Cool, huh?"

I turned to him, grinning. "Do you know what I like best about you?"

"Hard to say." He drew me close, eyes smiling. "There's so much to choose from."

I looped my arms around his neck. "That you still think things like this are cool. This is the best vacation ever, Miles. Thank you for making me come here."

"It hasn't even started yet," he pointed out, still smiling. "It only gets better from here."

"I'm going to hold you to that." I tilted my face up for the kiss I'd been waiting for, confident that was one promise he would have no trouble keeping. In the middle of paradise with two of my favorite people and my dog, what could possibly go wrong?

That was when I heard a woman's voice calling from outside the room, "Miles! Darling, are you there? It's me!"

CHAPTER THREE

Miles drew away from me slowly, a look of rather abashed resignation on his face. I simply stared at him, frozen in place. The voice came again, closer now.

"Miles?"

That voice definitely did not belong to Melanie.

"Come on," he said, taking my hand. "There's someone I want you to meet." And, raising his voice, he called out, "We're here, Mom!"

I was so shocked I actually stumbled as he pulled me forward.

I had never met Miles's mother, although I had talked to her briefly on the phone once or twice when she was babysitting Melanie. Perhaps because Melanie called her "Grandma", perhaps because I knew she had to be in her late sixties, I had always pictured a plump, pleasant, gray-haired woman in an apron. The woman who came into the room from the balcony could not have been further from what I imagined. She was slim and fit looking, with shoulder-length platinum hair, gorgeous cheekbones and sparkling green eyes. She wore a long watercolor chiffon beach caftan over her swimsuit and gold sandals with kitten heels. She came toward us with hands extended, a smile lighting up her whole face.

"Darling, you look wonderful! It's so good to see you!"

Miles caught her up in an embrace, lifting her off her feet, and she laughed and pounded his back. When he set her on her feet again, she turned to me, still beaming.

"And you're Raine," she said, and grasped both my hands warmly. "It's so good to finally meet you! I've already met your canine friend, and he's every bit as charming as Melanie described. He shook my hand with his paw!"

"I, um, it's nice to meet you, Mrs. Young," I managed.

"Rita," she insisted, and gave my hands a final squeeze before releasing them and turning back to Miles. "I set up drinks by the pool. Melanie has gone to change into her suit, she says you promised she could take the dog to the beach. Come down when you're ready," she added with an airy wave over her shoulder as she left the room. "So glad you're here, Raine!"

I hardly knew what to say, or to think. What kind of man brings his mother on vacation with his girlfriend? The same kind who brings his daughter, I supposed. But were we really at the stage where we spent family holidays together? What was it supposed to mean, that he would even take me to meet his mother, much less take me twelve hundred miles from home to spend a week with her? And why hadn't he told me? What kind of man *does* that?

Finally I managed, "Your mother is, um, nice."

"I thought you'd like her," he agreed easily. "She came in yesterday to open up the house. By the way, all the bedrooms share the balcony."

I tried very hard not to glare at him. Apparently I wasn't particularly successful, because he raised an admonishing finger and said, "Don't start."

My smile was stiff. "Start what?"

"Start with what does it mean when a guy invites his girl on vacation with his mother, are we ready for this, am I rushing things, blah blah. My mother is here because I like having her around and I thought it would be good to have someone to look after Melanie if you and I wanted some private time. End of story."

45

"I'm glad you invited her," I said, as genuinely as I possibly could. "But why didn't you tell me?"

"That one's easy." He kissed me lightly. "You never would have come if I had." He gave me a light pat on the bottom and added as he left, "Get changed. I'll see you downstairs."

I watched him go with a small incredulous shake of my head, then went to find my swimsuit. Even in paradise nothing was perfect, I supposed.

My green maillot swimsuit had last been worn white-water rafting down the Nantahala River, and was looking a little frayed around the seat. The only other swimsuit I owned was a cute little patchwork plaid bikini that I had bought a couple of years ago when I'd thought I might be able to get in some pool time while attending an Association of Pet Dog Trainers conference in Orlando. There was no way I was wearing that to have drinks with Miles's mother, so I put on the one piece and the only cover-up I had brought—a big white shirt that did what it was supposed to do but wasn't nearly as glamorous as the one Miles's mother had worn. I almost reconsidered a trip to one of those fancy shops downtown, but only for a moment. I packed my beach bag with bottled water and Cisco's folding travel bowl, pick-up bags, a dog towel and a people towel; sunscreen, a tennis ball, a floating flying disc, bug spray, dog treats, my phone, my camera, and a lightweight sand mat for Cisco to lie on. I grabbed my hat and sunglasses, hoisted the beach bag over my shoulder, and I was ready to go.

I had apparently dallied over my appearance longer than I had intended, because when I arrived poolside Miles and his mother had already settled into lounge chairs with drinks in their hands and Melanie was bouncing impatiently on the edge of her seat, Cisco's leash in her hand. Cisco, his fur still damp and rumpled, sat alertly in front of her with an expression of expectant anticipation in his eyes.

"There you are!" Melanie exclaimed, jumping up. "We've been *dying*!"

Cisco rushed over to greet me, and I knelt to give him a kiss, grateful for the distraction. "Sorry to keep you waiting, buddy," I said to him. I winked at Melanie. "You, too."

Miles said, "Lemonade or wine, Raine? We have some cheese and fruit too."

I stood up. "Nothing for me, thanks."

I was happy to see that Miles was not one of those middle-aged men who liked to show off his hard-won physique in a Speedo. Not that he wouldn't have looked great in one, but he looked even better in swim trunks and an open Hawaiian shirt. In fact, he looked so great that I really would have liked to see him without the shirt, tossing a flying disc for Cisco on the beach. But now I had a dilemma. Miles and his mother seemed to be settled in with drinks and snacks, and the polite thing to do of course would be to join them. But what I really wanted to do was go to the beach with Melanie and Cisco.

"We were just talking about what to do for dinner," Miles said.

I laughed a little. "We just had lunch!"

"I say we should stay in and let the service bring dinner," his mother said. "They make a wonderful poached fish... what's it called?"

"It's our first night here," Miles objected. "I want to take my girls out on the town. What are you in the mood for, Raine?"

"Really," I said, "I'm fine with whatever you decide."

"Daaaad," Melanie said, drawing out the word to emphasize her frustration. "Some of us have to go to bed at nine, you know. Any chance of getting in some beach time before bedtime?"

I couldn't help grinning, and Miles lifted his sunglasses to give his daughter a level look. "Would you like to try for eight?" he said, but I noticed his lips were twitching too.

Cisco picked up the leash that Melanie had dropped and made a soft whining sound in his throat. Both Miles and his mother laughed at that, and Miles swung his feet to the ground. "Okay, let's hit the beach. Did you put on plenty of sunscreen?"

Melanie assured him that she had, and then asked, "What about Cisco? Do dogs need sunscreen?"

I clipped on Cisco's leash and said, "Actually they do, especially if they have white coats or if their fur is really short. That's why it's sometimes a bad idea to shave your dog in the summer. They make a special spray for dogs. I'll put some on Cisco when we get down there."

Miles picked up my beach bag and lifted his eyebrows. "How long are you planning to be gone? Your luggage didn't weigh this much."

"Dogs need a lot of stuff," I replied defensively.

"Grandma, are you coming?" Melanie called.

"Right behind you, sweetheart. Miles, you forgot your phone."

Miles had one of those super-duper smart-phones with satellite technology—some of which I was pretty sure wasn't even on the market yet—that worked anywhere in the world. He had given Melanie and me one just like it and had probably given one to his mother too. There once was a time when I might have chided him for taking a phone like that on vacation. After all, did he *really* need to be able to reach Hong Kong from St. Bart's? But I knew better now. And I had my phone in my beach bag.

"Thanks." He took it from her and dropped it into his shirt pocket. "I'll make dinner reservations when we get down there."

There was a walk-through gate opposite the pool where a set of stone steps wound down the hillside fifty feet or so to the white sand below. It would be no easy climb under the best of circumstances and for safety's sake I decided it would be best if I handled Cisco's leash, at least on his first trip down. There was an electronic keypad set into the stone pillar at the side of the gate, and I watched Miles punch in a code.

"It's always the day's six-digit date," he explained to me. "Month, day and year followed by a code word. This week the code word is—"

"Cisco!" cried Melanie proudly.

He grinned. "We wanted it to be easy for you to remember," he told me. "If you get stranded on the beach, there's no other way in. And remember the code resets at midnight."

It seemed like an awful lot of security for paradise, but I supposed that was the way rich people lived. I said, "They do the same thing at the nursing home. The day of the week part, not the Cisco part. Seems to me like the hardest thing in a place like this would be remembering what day it is."

Miles's mother laughed. "You're right about that. That's why I find it easier never to leave the property."

The gate swung open and Melanie skipped through, scrambling down the steps without so much as a backward wave to us. Both Miles and his mother called after her, "Be careful!" and I was glad I hadn't succumbed to the same impulse. Cisco started to lunge after her, but I quickly brought him into a close heel as we started down the steps. Miles and his mother followed behind me, and the gate swung closed automatically.

"I didn't want to bring it up in front of Melanie," Miles's mother said, "but did you hear the awful news about Rachelle Denison?"

"The driver told us," Miles said. "He said the police had closed down the dive site."

"I should imagine so. They're still trying to recover the body from what I understand."

Cisco's eagerness had taken me two steps below them, but now I brought him to a halt and looked back. Miles's expression was as confused as mine, but I was still a little shy around his mother so I was glad that he asked the question. "What do you mean? I thought she was diving with her husband. How can they not have a body?"

"Oh, darling, I don't know." She took his arm for support and caught up the billowing skirt of her caftan in the other hand. "The whole thing is just so awful. Apparently there was some kind of equipment failure underwater, and he tried to help her get to the surface by sharing his oxygen, but something went wrong and he had to surface without her. Of course he kept diving and searching, but never found her. The poor man. They think she was caught in a current near one of the caves, although it seems to me so much time has passed that they're not likely to find anything now."

Miles sighed. "Let's try not to discuss this in front of Mel, okay? I don't want her to be afraid of the water. But I am glad she put off starting scuba lessons," he added.

"Good heavens." Her expression was not easy to read behind the oversized dark glasses, but the horror in her voice was unmistakable. "Scuba lessons? Out of the question! I wouldn't sleep a wink. For the rest of my life," she added pointedly, and Miles tightened one corner of his lips. Apparently they had had this argument before.

"At any rate," she went on, "her husband is a wreck, as you might well imagine. And that's what I wanted to mention. Someone by the name of Amanda Rickey called the house this morning. It seems some of his friends are getting together on

Wednesday evening at his house for a—not a memorial service exactly, but a show of support. Apparently they had all planned a big anniversary party for the Barrys and now it seems to have turned into a wake, if you can imagine anything so tacky. I suppose they didn't want to waste the catering. She wanted to know if we would come. Of course I didn't know the man at all, but I suppose you can hardly say no."

"How did she know Miles would be here?" I asked, holding on to my hat as a sea breeze flipped back the brim.

"It's a small island," Miles said with a shrug.

"And the concierge service has a list of all the people who are in town," his mother added. "That's what I would do if I were giving a party—I'd ask them for the list."

Miles said, "Party? You're right—tacky."

"Well, what can you expect? The people here are so strange. Give me my friends back in Myrtle Beach any day. They may be old and cranky, but at least they know how to act at a funeral."

I was starting to like her more and more. I said, "I don't want to sound ignorant, but I've never heard of her. Was she supposed to be famous?"

"Famous might be an exaggeration," Miles said. "Besides that vampire thing—"

"Werewolf," I corrected.

He shrugged. "She couldn't have had much of a career. My impression was that she was just starting out. She was only in her twenties. And yes," he added before I could ask, "her husband is my age. Maybe older. Definitely a trophy wife."

"Miles, please," his mother admonished.

"I was going to say gold digger," I said, "but it's not nice to speak ill of the dead."

"Thank you, Raine," said Rita—I really *had* to get used to calling her that, if only in my head. "My thoughts exactly."

"About the gold digger or the trophy wife?" Miles said, and at his mother's exclamation of exasperation he held up a hand of surrender. "Sorry. It's entirely possible she was a nice person and I'm sorry she's dead. No one deserves that. But I've known Alex Barry for years and I can assure you he's *not* a nice person. It's hard to be as sympathetic as I probably should be."

I turned to look at him over my shoulder. "Does that mean you're not going to the wake, or whatever it is?"

"Of course I'm going," he replied. "It's good business."

Rita shook her head in dismay. "Where did I go wrong?"

I tried not to smile. Like I said, I was really beginning to like her.

We had reached the bottom of the steps and Melanie, who had raced to the surf's edge, called, "Let him go! Let's play Frisbee!"

Cisco's ears were so far forward they were in danger of flying off his head, and his tail slammed back and forth against my legs.

I glanced at Miles. "Is it okay to let him off leash?"

"I don't see why not." He nodded toward a red-and-white striped pavilion a few feet away, where lounge chairs, a table and even a cooler were already set up. "That's our tent. I'll put your beach bag there."

"Wait." I dived my hand into the bag and dug out the flying disc and the tennis ball, then knelt to unclip Cisco's leash. He took off toward Melanie like a shot. "See ya!" I said to Miles and raced after my dog, fully prepared to have the time of my life.

"Glad you're learning to relax!" he called after me, and I barely spared him a wave as I splashed into the surf with Melanie and Cisco.

Melanie and I tossed the Frisbee back and forth and laughed out loud as Cisco bounded through the water and twisted in the air to catch it. Miles joined us for a time, tossing the ball into the surf for Cisco to chase. I loved watching Cisco paddle out and over the undulating waves, then dive under like a pelican and come up with the tennis ball in his mouth, amazing everyone. The four of us swam together for a time, jumping waves like children and letting the tide carry us to shore. Then Miles brought out a paddle board, which neither Melanie nor I had the patience to master on our first day out, so he took it out beyond the tide line while Melanie, Cisco and I went back to the tent for cold drinks and a fresh layer of sunscreen.

I was ready to relax and sit in the shade for awhile, but Cisco and Melanie were nowhere near that point. Rita suggested we look for seashells, which was the kind of clever compromise only a mother could come up with. I pulled on my cover-up and my hat and was content to walk at a leisurely pace along the shore line with Rita while Cisco and Melanie romped ahead.

There were other pavilions like ours on the beach with people sunbathing around them, and a few people swimming, kayaking or paddle-boarding in the sea, but for the most part the beach was quiet and relatively uncrowded. "This is not really a family-oriented beach," Rita explained. "Not like back home, anyway. But it's nice for a change, and Melanie seems to have a good time here."

"Little girls always have a good time when they're with their daddies," I pointed out, but even saying that caused a small hidden pain in my heart, which I quickly sealed off and pushed away. Not even my memories were untainted now.

"I suppose that's true," she answered with a small laugh. And then she glanced at me. "I want to thank you, Raine. Melanie is a different child now, and it's mostly because of you."

"Me?" I looked at her in surprise. "I didn't do anything."

"Of course you did. When Melanie lived with her mother…" She cut herself off with a small shake of her head. "Well, the less said about that the better, I suppose."

I had never met Melanie's mother, who had abandoned her daughter—literally—last year to live in Brazil with her new husband, surrendering custody to Miles in the process. She still texted and talked to Melanie on the phone, and Melanie seemed pretty sanguine about the whole thing, but I would never understand how a mother could do that—just walk away from her daughter for the sake of a man.

Anymore than I could understand how a man could betray his family for the sake of a woman.

"Anyway," Rita went on, "that situation was definitely not the best, and I'm afraid my granddaughter was growing up to be a bit of a brat."

I diplomatically said nothing.

"But then she met you, and when you gave her the puppy, everything changed. I really don't know if she would have made it through the whole transition after her mother left if it hadn't been for that little dog."

"Puppies always change things," I agreed, "and almost always for the better."

"It gave her a purpose bigger than herself," said Rita, "and made her feel important. But even more than the puppy, I don't think Melanie had ever had a strong female role model before. You gave her that, and that's why I wanted to meet you, and thank you." She reached out and gave my arm a little squeeze, smiling. "So thank you."

Wow. I had never been anyone's role model before. Certainly I had never thought about Melanie and myself in those terms. The only thing I knew about modeling any kind of behavior was in relationship to dogs: if you respect them, they respect you back. If you listen to them, they will listen to you. If you remain calm and confident, they will be relaxed and secure. Come to think of it, a lot of the same things pretty much applied to children as well.

Still, I felt awkward. "I didn't even like kids until I met Melanie," I admitted. "She's something special."

"So she is," agreed her grandmother indulgently. "And she's completely crazy about you and Cisco. Miles is too, of course, although I suspect in his case Cisco definitely takes second place."

"Oh," I said, feeling tongue-tied and inarticulate. "Well, I'm crazy about them, too." I could feel my face go a shade of red that had nothing to do with the hours I'd spent in the sun.

"Oh dear," Rita said. "Now I've done exactly what I promised Miles I wouldn't do. I've embarrassed you. Promise you won't tell."

I was somewhere between delighted and intrigued. "Miles asked you not to embarrass me?"

"Wait." Her expression went thoughtful. "Maybe it was not to embarrass *him*."

I laughed, and it was official: I really liked Miles's mom.

Which, if I thought about it, only opened up a whole new set of problems.

I did not have time to think about anything right then, however, because at that moment a big wet golden retriever came bounding up, tongue lolling, tail spiraling, spraying us with sand and salt as he barreled between us, did a quick 360, and raced the other way again. "Cisco!" I exclaimed.

But no sooner was the word out of my mouth than another golden— just as wet, just as sandy and just as big—dashed between us, almost knocking Rita off her feet. I could hear Melanie's laughter in the background, and a male voice calling, "Cocoa! Cocoa, you bad dog!"

I caught Rita's arm to steady her as the two dogs raced away from us. "Are you okay?"

"Good heavens," she said, pushing her sunglasses back into place. "Was that Cisco?"

The two dogs were running toward us again, followed by Melanie, who was followed by a dark-haired young man in khaki shorts and a white tee shirt. He called again, "Cocoa! Cocoa, I'm going to wring your neck! Come here, you rotten dog!"

If I were a dog, I would have come.

I stepped forward, raised my arm for attention, and called in a clear, don't-mess-with-me-now voice, "Cisco, come!"

I should add that I said a little prayer, as I always did, that this time he would listen. And he did.

One of the wet goldens swiveled his ears toward me, did a minor course correction, and galloped to an attentive sit at my feet. I reached into the pocket of my cover-up for a treat—seriously, every garment I own has greasy hot-dog stains on it—and exclaimed, "Good dog!" as I popped the treat into his mouth.

Usually, around this time the other dog would realize that something about Cisco's behavior had generated a treat and would try to imitate it. This dog was out of control. He galloped around me, bumped my hands for a treat, reared up on his hind legs as though to jump on me, and only when I folded my arms and turned my back did he finally give up. Cisco regarded him impatiently as he came to a stop before me and sniffed my hands until, having determined something else was required, he sat beside Cisco. I said, "Good dog!" and produced another treat from my pocket. I'm never without them.

Melanie came running up, out of breath and laughing. "Look, Raine, Cisco made a friend! They're like brothers or something."

"I am so sorry!" The young man who had been chasing his dog arrived on Melanie's heels. "He's a little headstrong."

"That's okay," I said, smiling. "I'm familiar with the syndrome."

The two dogs, sensing no more treats were forthcoming, got up and started sniffing the ground. I gave Cisco a sharp, "Ank!" in reprimand, and he immediately sat again. In my house, we practice the implied stay, which means that whenever I give a command, the dog should continue doing it until I tell him otherwise. Of course, the trick to making this effective is to make corrections last for only seconds, and as Cisco's butt hit the ground, I said, "Release!", and he went off to join his friend in sniffing for more treats.

"I wish I could get this knucklehead to do that," said the young man with a grin, ruffling his dog's ears. "I hope he didn't bother you."

Rita said, "You're American. It's nice to hear a familiar accent."

"Canadian, actually." He extended his hand. "I'm Rick, and that's Cocoa."

We introduced ourselves and shook hands all around. "Maybe they can have play dates," Melanie suggested hopefully. "Cisco and Cocoa, I mean." She watched as one of the dogs tagged the other on the tail and a quick game of chase-and-tumble began. Honestly, at a distance I couldn't tell which was which. They even wore the same red collar.

"That would be great," said Rick, "but Cocoa isn't really my dog. He belongs to the family I work for. I just take care of him. We run on the beach every day about this time though. Maybe he and Cisco can play together again."

"Cool," Melanie said, and looked at me. "Let's remember that, okay, Raine? Cisco needs to play with friends his own age."

I could hardly keep from laughing, and I could tell Rita was struggling too. I assured her, "I think you're right. But now we'd better start back before your father sends out a search party. It was nice meeting you and Cocoa, Rick," I told the young man. "And the trick to getting a dog to come is sliced hot dogs, dehydrated in the microwave for five or ten seconds."

He grinned. "Hey, thanks. Maybe we'll see you tomorrow. Come on, Cocoa."

He caught Cocoa's collar and turned to go back up the beach. The dog fell happily into step beside him until Melanie said, "Cisco, come on, let's go home."

The dog with Rick turned and looked back at us alertly. The dog Melanie had addressed as Cisco ignored her.

I said, "Um…"

Rick released Cisco's collar and he bounced back to us, grinning and looking for more treats. I slipped my hand under Cocoa's collar and brought him forward. "I think this is your dog," I said.

"Man, sorry about that." He quickly came forward and took Cocoa's collar. "I'd lose my job if I brought home the wrong dog. " He gave us another quick grin and a wave. "Have a good day, now!"

He took off at a jog down the beach, and this time Cocoa followed him. I held on to Cisco's collar so he would not.

Rita watched the young man go, a thoughtful expression her face. "Canadian, my big toe," she said, and that made Melanie giggle. "Did you hear the way he pronounced 'dog'? One 'o', not two. I'll bet my last dime that young man has never been north of Washington D.C. in his life."

She might have been right about the accent, but I had to admit I'd never been able to tell the difference between a Canadian accent and, say, a Minnesotan one. We didn't get much of either in Western North Carolina. I said, "Why would he lie?"

She shrugged, but Melanie suggested, "Maybe his boss is French. They hate Americans."

That made us both laugh a little, mostly in surprise at her perspicuity, and Rita said, "That's as good an explanation as any. You're pretty smart for a little kid, you know that?'

Melanie agreed easily, "I know."

We turned back toward the pavilion, and Melanie and Cisco raced ahead. I hadn't thought about it much until Rita pointed it out, but Melanie had changed a lot in the past six months—from a sullen, smart-mouthed kid addicted to video games and electronic devices to a bright young girl who was focused and disciplined, curious and outgoing, who loved the outdoors and was well on her way to becoming one heck of a dog handler—not to mention a pretty good detective, which she currently insisted was her future profession. I refused to believe that I was responsible for all of that, of course, but it made me feel a little proud to think I might have had even a small part in bringing it out.

Melanie was regaling her father with the story of Cisco's new friend when we reached the pavilion. Cisco was lapping up water from his folding canvas bowl—so tired that he was doing so lying down, I noticed—and Miles had made room for his daughter on the padded chaise beside him, his phone in his hand. "We're here for the rest of the week," he teased her. "You and Cisco don't have to do everything on the first day. By the way," he told us as I sank into the chair beside him, "we have dinner reservations at seven. That's early for the in crowd, but I know a place or two that doesn't even open until midnight if you want to go clubbing later."

He managed to say this with a straight face, and I gave it the response it deserved. I leaned back in the chair, pulled my hat down over my eyes, and said, "Have fun." I had been up since four thirty that morning and I wasn't even sure I could make it through dinner.

Melanie said thoughtfully, "Say, do you think Cocoa *could* be Cisco's brother?"

"Could be," I murmured without opening my eyes. "Cisco comes from a pretty famous line." But that was another thing I didn't want to think about. The line that Cisco came from had been developed in part by Maude. She had given me my first golden retriever, from whom Cisco was descended. Maude had been such a major part of my life for so many years. And for most of those years, she had been lying to me.

Melanie said, "What's his kennel name again?"

I opened my eyes as she picked up her father's phone. "Melanie, I don't think…"

"I'm just going to look up his litter. Wouldn't it be cool to know where all the puppies went?"

"Well…"

"Hey, Dad." She turned the phone around to him. "Google alert."

Miles took the phone and glanced at it. He sat up straighter, murmuring, "Well, I'll be—"

He cut himself off, and both Rita and I turned to look at him. "Rachelle Denison's death is now being called a homicide," he told us, "and Alex Barry is being questioned for murder."

CHAPTER FOUR

So much for not discussing Rachelle Denison's drowning in front of Melanie, although I have to hand it to Miles, he did a pretty good job of being both straightforward and brief— possibly because there was nothing more to tell—and Melanie soon lost interest. What he did not mention, and I was dying to ask, was why he had set up a Google alert in the first place.

I was not to have a chance to satisfy my curiosity that afternoon, though. Cisco had to be shampooed, sun-dried, brushed out and fed, and by the time I got my own curly hair shampooed and tamed and had changed into a floral-print sundress with cute yellow sandals that I admit I bought just for the trip, I was the last one down. Both Cisco and I enjoyed the outdoor shower, though.

Miles was on the lanai, looking very dapper in a custom-tailored sports jacket and an open-throated white shirt, and very serious as he talked on the phone. I was little annoyed at this, as I had hoped he would be able to put business on hold at least for the time we were here, and so far he'd done a pretty good job. No one was perfect, I supposed. However, he disconnected immediately and was back in vacation mode the minute Melanie called, "Dad, we're ready! Let's go!"

I loved the place Miles had chosen, mostly because it was clear he had done so with Melanie in mind. It was like walking into a rain forest, with tumbling waterfalls at every turn and curtains of greenery separating one table from the next. There was a sky-high central atrium with a glass roof and a parrot cage that went from floor to ceiling. Every table had a view of the colorful soaring birds, and I was just as fascinated by them as Melanie was. Rita and I had some kind of rainbow-layered drink that we both discovered midway through was far too strong to finish, and Melanie had a watermelon-lime non-alcoholic cocktail that she claimed was delicious.

I enjoyed listening to Rita and Miles remember the old days and tell stories about each other—some of them mildly embarrassing, some just fun. And because Melanie had never heard those stories either, I felt like part of the family. Miles encouraged me to try a sushi appetizer—seriously, we don't get much sushi in Hansonville—which was surprisingly good, and the fish *en croute* that I had for a main course was unbelievable. When Melanie and her grandmother excused themselves between the main course and dessert to go to the ladies' room, I took the opportunity to scoot around the semi-circular banquette seat and kiss Miles quickly on the cheek.

"This," I told him, "has been a perfect day. Thank you."

"You're welcome." But when I started to slide away again he caught my fingers, eyes twinkling. "Say it."

"Say what?"

"You know what."

From somewhere inside that still existed from the pre-vacation Raine, I found a mildly annoyed frown. "You were right," I mumbled.

"Excuse me? Couldn't quite catch that."

I gave a sigh of exasperation. "I said you were right, okay? I needed to get away. You were right."

He smiled. "So I was." He kissed my fingers. "And I'm glad you're having a good time."

I smiled at him and started to slide back to my own seat again but he held on to my fingers.

"Hey," he said. "Have I told you how good you look here?"

A surprised blush tinged my already sun-burnished cheeks. "Thanks," I said, trying to brush it off. "It's the lighting."

"Not just here," he said, holding my gaze, "but *here* . On the island. In the sunshine. In a swimsuit. At a sidewalk café. Playing with Mel. Talking to Mom. I'm glad you're here."

I knew what he meant. I *felt* good here. I had thought I wouldn't, I'd thought I would be completely at odds and out of my element here and in a way I suppose I was but at the same time it felt good. I felt good. I knew what he meant and I liked it, I just didn't know how to respond to it.

I'm sure I would have thought of something, though, if at that moment my thoughts hadn't been shattered by a gushing female voice declaring, "Miles! Darling!"

Seriously? Again?

This time when I looked up I did not see Miles's mother, but a gorgeous redhead in a décolletage-baring beach dress with a long, flowing skirt and an empire waist—exactly the kind of dress I had always pictured myself wearing if I were starring in a romantic movie that featured a beach scene. Miles stood, and she kissed him—if not exactly on the lips, a little too close for my taste.

"Stephanie," he said. "It's good to see you." He turned to me. "This is—"

"Number Four, I know," she interrupted, eyeing me with amusement. "Not your usual type, darling."

I knew she was referring to Miles's ex-wives, of which he only had three to my knowledge. I reached around him and extended my hand, my smile completely false. "I'm Raine," I told her. "I don't have a number."

She lifted an eyebrow, took my hand in a limp grip, and then turned back to Miles, dismissing me. "It's been ages. We've all missed you. What in the world have you been up to?"

"This and that," he returned. He remained standing, a clear signal he did not intend to prolong the conversation, which was definitely a good thing. "What about you? Is Jackson here with you?"

"Oh, please." She gave a dismissive wave of her hand. "I divorced that sniveling excuse for a man last year. Did you hear what happened?" She leaned in close, giving both of us a preferred-seating view of her perfectly harnessed breasts, along with a cloud of perfume that was too exotic for me to name. She widened her eyes and lowered her voice confidentially, drawing an invisible circle that included only Miles and herself. "We were at our house in Grosse Point when we woke up to a man with a knife standing right over our bed! And can you imagine—can you just *imagine* —what Jackson did? He started crying. He begged for mercy. And then he ripped the diamond ring right off my finger and gave it to the thief! Well, of course I knew right then it was over between us. I filed for divorce the next day."

Miles murmured something sympathetic, but I couldn't help noticing his expression was bored. Perhaps Stephanie noticed as well because she straightened up and went on, "Of course, it's really no better here. Six robberies this season alone and of course you heard about poor Rachelle. And the police here are so incompetent all they can think to do is blame Alex! How ridiculous is that? Susan is here, I know she'll be glad you are too. She came in for the anniversary party but now… what a tragedy. It will be a wake instead." She brightened. "Maybe we can all get together for dinner."

Miles said politely, "My schedule is uncertain."

She looked briefly confused, then smiled brightly, getting the message. "Well, lovely to see you. I'm here for the week. I'll see you at Alex's Wednesday, I hope?"

Miles just smiled and answered, "You never know."

She glanced in my direction, then back at Miles. "Keep in touch, won't you darling? Nice to meet you, Storm."

"Raine."

"Right. Bye, Miles."

When she was gone I lost no time resuming my seat on the opposite side of the booth, and Miles sat down, regarding me mildly. "Don't look at me like that," he said. "If I ever wake up to man standing over the bed with a knife, I'm counting on you to protect me."

I said, "Please tell me you didn't date her."

"Okay." He lifted his club soda, his expression completely unreadable, and took a sip. "I didn't date her."

I couldn't help frowning as I tried to decide whether that might be true. "Who is Susan?"

"Alex Barry's sister."

Another woman, I supposed, that he hadn't dated. If I was the jealous type, which I totally am not—at least under most circumstances— I could have pursued that, but there was something else that interested me more. "Miles," I said, "why did you set up a Google alert for Rachelle Denison? I thought you wanted to keep the whole thing out of the family vacation."

"Three hundred eighty six thousand dollars," he responded.

My brows shot up in surprise and confusion. "What?"

But just then Melanie returned with an excited report about the underwater murals that were painted on the ladies' room walls, and shortly after that dessert arrived. Melanie started to wind down over her chocolate sundae, and by the end of it could barely keep her eyes open. I knew how she felt. But as tired as I was my day was never done until my dog's day was done, and from the way Cisco greeted us at the door, dancing and circling and doing all his tricks for attention, I knew he had gotten his second wind.

Miles volunteered to go with me as I announced my intention to take Cisco for a quick walk on the beach, which suited me just fine. The grounds were illuminated with magical landscape lighting that turned the pool into a shimmering sheet of silk and the palm trees into mystical towers of shadow and light. It was all so gorgeous I wanted to linger, but the sandy shore and the sound of the ocean beckoned. The steps were inset with safety lighting, and we descended three abreast, pausing midway down to take in the view—the indigo sea, the distant lights of a yacht at anchor, the sky peppered with stars. There really is nothing in this world more romantic than a walk on a tropical beach under a starlit sky with the guy you're crazy about. The ocean was whispering and sighing all around, tropical breezes tugging at my air and playing with my skirt, warm damp sand between my toes. Of course, with Cisco along, it was a bit less romantic than either of us might have liked, but still it was nice, just the three of us on the beach, Miles's arm around my waist, Cisco at my side. Besides, I had unfinished business.

I left my sandals at the bottom of the stairs and we walked for awhile with nothing but the sound of the ocean and the rattling of the palms for company. The other villas on the hill provided the only source of light, and I was not comfortable letting Cisco off lead in the dark. I put him in "free walk" mode so that he could wander to the end of the leash and sniff the sand to his heart's content. After a time I said, "Three hundred eighty six thousand dollars?"

Miles did not pretend to misunderstand. "The amount I contracted for with Alex Barry's company last year to install the security systems in my new buildings. I thought it might be a good idea to keep an eye on my investment, so I set up the Google alert for his name."

"Security?" I said. "He's in security?"

"Altmore Security, one of the biggest providers of home and business security in the U.S."

"Whoa," I said. "Bad news for Altmore Security, with its owner being questioned for murder, and all."

"Precisely," agreed Miles, and there was a grim note to his tone that caused me to look up at him in concern. In the dark, though, it was hard to tell how upset he was, if at all. "I'm sure I'm not the only client who's wondering what else he's capable of, and if enough people bail—or sue—there goes the business, along with the cash his clients paid for services not provided."

"Wow, Miles, I'm sorry," I said, horrified at the thought of anyone, much less someone I knew, losing that much money. "I had no idea."

He gave my waist a reassuring squeeze, smiling down at me in the dark. "It's not that big a deal for me financially, but nobody likes to be ripped off. I have an investigator for things like this, and he's looking into the case against Alex now. He should have some answers for me tomorrow."

I was still trying to get my mind around the fact that a three hundred thousand dollar loss was not that big a deal for Miles when something else occurred to me. I frowned. "I'm curious," I said.

"I'm not surprised."

"You said this afternoon you'd known Alex Barry for years and he was not a nice person. So why did you hire him?"

He chuckled softly. "Honey, if I only did business with nice people I'd be in business by myself. He's good at what he does, that's why."

"Do you think he's capable of murder?"

He hesitated just a fraction of a second too long. "I think anyone's capable of murder, given the right circumstances."

Funny. That's what my ex-husband, the current sheriff of Hanover County, always said.

"But," I pointed out, peering up at him, "you think he's involved in his wife's death. You thought so even when it was still being called an accident."

He hesitated for only a moment before admitting, "Honey, I've dived those caves and believe me, they are one of the least likely spots in the world for a deadly accident. Tourists play there, for God's sake. As for the body disappearing…" I could feel his shrug. "It could happen, I guess, but I don't think I've ever heard of it in all the time I've been coming here."

"Apparently the police agree with you," I murmured.

We stopped for Cisco to sniff a pile of seaweed, and Miles blew out a breath. "This," he said, "is exactly what I didn't want. Vacation, remember? Enough about me. Let's talk about you."

And with that he took Cisco's leash, turned me in his arms, and we didn't talk about anything at all for a very long time. There is definitely something about a star-tossed tropical night on the beach with a man who knows how to put that night to its best use that can drive all thoughts of crime, criminals and murder plots out of a girl's head.

We walked back to the house with fingers entwined, my head resting on Miles's shoulder, and Cisco meandering along a few feet ahead of us. "Snorkeling tomorrow?" Miles murmured into my hair.

"Hmm. Sounds great."

"We'll have to stop in town to pick up a life vest for Cisco."

If anyone ever wonders what I see in Miles— and there are days when I wonder that myself, a lot—there's the answer. Not the canine life vest for a family sailing trip. But because he considered Cisco family. Simple.

We were halfway up the steps when I stopped. "Oh, Miles. I left my shoes on the beach." I might not have worried about them, but they were brand new, and my favorite.

Miles handed Cisco's leash to me. "Go on up, I'll get them. Remember the code?"

"Unless it's after midnight," I responded, and checked my watch just to be sure as he started down the stairs.

As soon as we started up the stairs again Cisco's ears swiveled forward and he bounded to the end of the leash. Since that was his usual greeting behavior, I assumed Melanie must still be up, waiting for us by the pool. If I had thought about it I would have noticed the lights were off in the house and remembered that both Melanie and Rita had announced their intentions of going straight to bed before we left, but all I did was speak sharply to Cisco for pulling and draw him back to my side. He stayed there, though with obvious reluctance, the rest of the climb up the stairs.

The landscape lighting provided plenty of illumination, but the keypad at the gate was also backlit, which made it easy to punch in the first three digits of the date. And then, for absolutely no reason, Cisco started to growl. I looked down at him, wondering what kind of island wildlife had scurried across the shadows to spook him, and then realized that anything that would scare Cisco was probably not something I wanted to meet in my bare feet. I gave his leash another wind around my hand and turned quickly back to the keypad. Abruptly, Cisco's growl escalated into a series of quick, throaty barks. That was when the whole world went dark.

I whirled around just as Cisco leapt to the end of his leash, almost pulling me off my feet in the process. I cried, "Hey!" and stumbled forward—into something solid. Something that pushed back. Cisco was escalating into a frenzy of excited barking and leaping; I flailed for balance and crashed backward into the gate. I heard Miles call, "Raine? You okay?" and I hauled Cisco back to me with both hands. I could have sworn I saw a shadow disappear into the deeper shadows of the dune a few feet away in that split second before the lights came back on, and then Miles was there, steadying me on my feet again.

I demanded, "Did you push me?"

"What?"

I peered into the shadows of the dunes that led toward the beach, but saw nothing. "I thought someone was here. Cisco started barking, and then I bumped into something…"

Almost before I finished speaking, Miles had punched in the key code, pushed Cisco and me through the gate, and thrust my shoes at me. "Stay here," he commanded.

"Hey!"

But the gate slammed with me on the wrong side of it, and Miles moved cautiously into the dunes. I saw the beam of a flashlight, and realized he had activated the flashlight app on his phone. I put Cisco in a sit stay and started re-entering the key code, but by the time I finished the flashlight beam was returning to me. I opened the gate for Miles.

There was a small line between his brows but he did not look overly concerned as he turned off the phone. "I didn't see anyone," he said. "The sand was scuffed up but people have been all over this property the past couple of days, tending the grounds and cleaning the pool...are you sure you saw someone?"

"No," I admitted. "It was pitch-black. I couldn't see my hand in front of my face. It's just that Cisco was pretty excited, and I could have sworn somebody bumped into me."

Cisco was snuffling at something on the ground, and I bent quickly to pick it up before he could. It was just a bag of hot dog treats that I must have dropped that afternoon. I tossed it into the trash can by the gate that was designated for beach trash. "What about the lights?"

"Power failure," he said. "We get them all the time here. The generator kicks in after ten seconds. Still, maybe I'd better—"

There was a sudden commotion in the bushes a few feet away and we both spun toward it. Cisco gave a whoop of alarm and then burst into startled barking as a big white bird whirred up from the ground and soared away. Both Miles and I laughed in relief.

"Well, there's your intruder," Miles said.

I knelt to comfort Cisco, who looked both disappointed and mildly embarrassed. "Guess so," I said, rubbing Cisco's neck briskly. "Good boy, though. You're on the job." I stood. "I hope we didn't wake everybody in the neighborhood."

"Honey, everybody in this neighborhood except us is just now getting dressed for dinner." He crooked his finger under my chin and tilted my face upwards for a kiss. "I, on the other hand, prefer an early bedtime."

I liked the way his eyes gleamed when he said that, and I settled happily into the crook of his arm as we started back toward the house.

I awoke the next morning to the whooshing of the ocean outside my window, a gentle yellow sunlight pressing against my closed eyelids, and the weight of a warm body next to mine. For a moment I thought it must be a delicious dream and I tried to settle back into sleep, and then I felt the pressure of someone's gaze, watching me. I cracked open one eye cautiously.

Melanie sat cross-legged on the bed beside me, wearing her swimsuit and a Batman tee shirt, her expression impatient. "Hey," she said.

I responded, "Hey," and turned over on my back, plumping the pillows beneath my head.

"Dad said to tell you he took Cisco for a run on the beach."

I yawned. "That's nice."

"Grandma's making crepes for breakfast, with croissants from the bakery in town."

Crepes? Now I was awake.

"And there's a woman downstairs looking for Dad. I thought you'd want to know."

I sat up, pushing back my hair. "Do you know who she is?"

"Nope." She slid off the bed and stood up. "I'll keep an eye on her for you, but if I were you I wouldn't waste any time. See you at the pool."

I was dressed and downstairs less than five minutes later.

I found Rita and Melanie sitting at the table beneath the shade pavilion by the pool. The table was set with colorful crockery and glasses of juice, a silver carafe of coffee and something wonderful-smelling beneath a domed platter. With them was a woman in a crisp white shirt, cropped designer jeans and bright red stiletto heels. She was one of those women who proved the adage that "forty was the new thirty", with expensively groomed butterscotch colored hair that brushed her shoulders, salon-maintained nails, and flawlessly applied makeup. Melanie, as promised, was watching the newcomer as though she expected her to try to steal the silver.

I approached the table and said, in my usual cheerful fashion, "Good morning, everyone." Okay, perhaps my tone was more guarded than cheerful, but my intentions were good.

The strange woman turned around at the sound of my voice. Rita, looking a little flustered, said, "Raine, Good morning. Susan, this is our friend Raine Stockton. Raine, this is Susan Barry."

Her smile was weak and distracted, and when I moved forward to offer my hand I noticed she barely glanced at me. I was getting used to that from the women in Miles's past. Her fingers were cold and boney, but her grip was firm as she shook my hand.

"You're Alex Barry's sister," I said, puzzled by what she was doing here.

"Also," she said with a faintly apologetic smile, "Miles's ex wife."

CHAPTER FIVE

Melanie put down the croissant she had been about to bite into and stared at the woman with renewed interest. "Whoa," she said. "I didn't see that coming."

Ditto that.

"I was just apologizing to Rita for barging in on your breakfast," she said while I just stood there feeling, and probably looking, like an idiot. "I hoped to catch Miles for just a minute before he left on his run. I should have called first."

I was finally able to move my gaze away from her and toward Rita, who looked just as uncomfortable, and probably even more confused, than I was. She said, "Coffee, Raine?"

I managed to find my way to a chair at the table without tripping over my own feet, and I sat down, accepting the cup of coffee Rita passed to me.

Melanie said to Susan curiously, "So which one are you?"

Susan responded politely, "I'm sorry?"

"Wife," Melanie clarified. "Which wife?"

"Second," Susan replied.

Melanie nodded sagely. "I'm his only child. He doesn't talk much about the other wives."

Susan took a breath, and got to her feet. "I'm sorry," she said, "I shouldn't have come. It's been a dreadful few days. Tell Miles I was by, will you? She reached into her tiny clutch purse and took out a card. "Here's my number."

Rita reached for the card uncertainly, clearly torn between curiosity, the good manners that should insist Susan join us for breakfast, and relief that she was leaving. I had an uneasy feeling that good manners were about to win out when the day was saved by the sound of scrabbling claws on teak. A wet golden retriever bounded around the corner, tongue lolling happily, leaving a trail of damp sand and paw prints behind. I drew a breath for another one of those magical emergency "halt!" commands before his excitement over seeing a stranger ruined Susan's designer jeans—not to mention our breakfast—but before I could get the syllable out, Susan exclaimed, "Cocoa!"

For a moment she looked oddly nonplussed, even disbelieving, then she bent to greet him, arms open. Of course Cisco galloped right to her, grinning with delight at the prospect of being showered with the affection he so richly deserved. The next words, even though they were accompanied by affectionate pats and ear rubs, were probably not what he expected. "Cocoa, you bad dog! Where have you been? Do you know how worried we were? How did you get here, anyway?"

I stood up, scraping my chair on the deck. "Um, that's not Cocoa," I said.

She looked at me as though she wanted to argue, but by this time I had discovered that Rita had also made sausages, and I commanded clearly, "Cisco, come."

Never in his life had that command not been followed, at some point, by a treat, so for Cisco the choice between the pleasant stranger with nice pats and the woman who held the sausage was a no-brainer. He raced toward me and skidded to a sit with his toes touching mine. Then, because I couldn't resist showing off, I said simply, "Finish." And Cisco flipped his rear quarters around in a semi-circle to sit at my left side. I fed Cisco the sausage, piece by piece.

Melanie grinned. There was definitely a note of superiority in her tone as she said to Susan, "I'll bet Cocoa can't do *that*."

But our moment of triumph was short-lived. Miles came around the corner then, his shoulders and short, spiky hair still gleaming with droplets of water, a towel around his neck. He was wearing running shorts but no shoes, and I presumed he had stopped at the beach shower to rinse off before coming to greet us, sending Cisco ahead. He stopped when he saw Susan, and the confusion on her face melted into relief when she saw him. She said simply, "Miles." The word was like a sigh.

After a moment in which whatever emotions he might be experiencing were masked by the sun in his mirror-gray eyes, he came forward, took her hands, and kissed her cheek. He said, "Hi, Susan. I heard you were here. I was sorry to hear about Rachelle."

She nodded mutely, and it seemed to me she held onto his hands a moment longer than necessary. "It's been a nightmare," she said. "I still can't believe it. And now the police are questioning Alex, and the press is camped outside the gate…"

Miles gave her an understanding nod and managed to extricate his hands, gesturing her toward the table. "Come have some coffee. Have you met everyone?"

She said, "Yes. But I can't stay." Her voice was tight, her expression urgent. "Miles, I need a favor."

Melanie demanded suspiciously, "How do you know Cocoa?"

She managed a brief smile for the sake of the daughter of the man from whom she was about to ask a favor. "There's only one golden retriever on the beach," she said, "or at least I thought there was. Cocoa is—was—Rachelle's dog." She squeezed her eyes closed and gave her head a tiny shake. Her voice was almost inaudible as she said, "That's hard to say. It doesn't seem real."

Miles touched her shoulder in a light gesture of comfort. How many times had he done the same to me? He said to Melanie, "So that was the dog you met yesterday. It makes sense. The Barry estate is just a quarter mile down the beach."

"Anyway, Cocoa got away from his handler this morning and has the whole house in an uproar, as if it wasn't already. He's probably home by now. I'm sorry I thought he was your dog. I can't believe how much they look alike."

Melanie rested a proprietorial hand on Cisco's head. "Cisco isn't my dog," she told Susan in a tone that implied she was not only an interloper, but an ill-informed one as well. "My dog is named Pepper and she's at home in Atlanta. Cisco is Raine's dog."

Miles led Susan to the table with his hand still resting lightly on her shoulder. "Come sit down. Tell me what you need."

And that's when I knew I didn't want to be there anymore. I said, "I'd better get Cisco cleaned up before he gets sand all over everything."

But before I could reach for Cisco's collar Melanie sprang up from the table and pushed in front of me. "I'll do it!" she volunteered.

I gave her a stern meaningful look but she replied with a big-eyed, Melanie Girl Spy tilt of her head toward the interloper, clearly indicating that I should not under any circumstances give up my ground. Since I was now trapped between Melanie and Cisco, there was no way I could.

"You didn't finish your breakfast," Rita objected.

"All done. Thank you, Grandma." She reached for Cisco's collar.

"And?" prompted Miles.

"And may I please be excused from the table?"

Her grandmother murmured, "I suppose." And, as she watched Miles seat his ex-wife next to the place that had been set for me, she looked as though she wished she, too, could ask to be excused. I knew the feeling.

Nonetheless, I watched Melanie skip off with Cisco in tow and slid into the chair between Rita and Susan. Susan smiled at Miles. "I never pictured you as a father. You're good at it."

Miles poured coffee for her, and then for himself. When he set the pot on the table again, I filled my own cup. He sat down and regarded Susan in a friendly, if cautious, manner. "It's been a long time," he said.

I did dearly hope they were not about to start reminiscing. I grabbed the fruit bowl and plopped a spoonful of chopped mangoes and kiwis on my plate, then offered the bowl to Susan with a smile so saccharine it should have rotted my teeth. "Have some?"

She replied with a brusque shake of her head and looked nervously at her coffee cup, fingering the handle. I helped myself to a generous serving of warm crepes dusted with cinnamon sugar from the domed platter. Miles seemed content to just watch Susan, patiently and without judgment, until she was ready to speak.

How many times had he looked at me like that?

Susan took a breath. "You know Alex and I have never been all that close," she said. "But Rachelle...we got to be friends. I don't know, I guess it was because we were both based in Los Angeles, and while Alex was flying off here and there on business we started hanging out."

Rita inquired pleasantly, "What do you do in Los Angeles, dear?"

"I'm a television producer," she answered, "for an entertainment news show. That's how I got to know Rachelle, really. She did a guest segment on our show for *Wolftown*, and she wasn't nearly as vapid and empty-headed as she'd seemed at the wedding. I liked her. She wasn't what you'd expect. Not a spoiled rich kid, not one of those air-head actresses. She was young, but smart. She didn't think she was a very good actress, and..." she made a small, wry expression with the corner of her lips, "the truth was, she wasn't. But she wanted to get better. She took lessons, and even though she probably could have bought her way into any movie she wanted she wanted to pay her dues. So she took parts in low-budget films--you know, the kind where the heroine in the cat suit kicks zombie ass, or shoots down terrorist planes with shoulder-missiles, or gets thrown off tall buildings by a serial killer or stalked by a maniacal babysitter—and television sitcoms and bad pilots. She would have thought this..." she gave a small shake of her head, "was just another bad script. The tragedy is that she'd just gotten a part in a major film, the kind that was life-changing, according to her. She was so excited about it, and the thing she was proudest of was that she'd earned it, nobody had given it to her. I think she finally thought she was living up to the family legacy. We had lunch the day before she left and it was all she could talk about. She said it felt as though her whole life was starting over."

She looked at Miles. "She was a good diver, Miles, and an incredible swimmer. She told me she actually had ambitions for the Olympic swim team in college. I can't believe she'd die in a diving accident in St. Bart's."

I said, "Are you saying you don't think it was an accident?" Even when I was mad, I couldn't control my curiosity. And make no mistake about it, I was mad.

She shook her head without glancing at me. "I don't know what I'm saying. Because Alex is a good diver too—you know that, Miles, you've dived with him—and he was the only one with her."

Miles said, "Who else was on the boat?"

"No one. It was going to be a night dive, so they took Alex's boat out to the reef around sunset. No one else was diving."

Rita said, "Forgive my ignorance, but why would anyone want to dive at night? Is that something people actually do?"

My question exactly. But, because I was making a big show of pretending to enjoy my crepes—which I'm sure were delicious, had I been able to taste them—I was glad Rita had asked it first.

Miles answered, "There's lots of phosphorescent plankton and small sea life that can be spectacular at night. And you can get some great underwater shots with the right camera. Also…"

"It's romantic," Susan supplied. "I probably shouldn't say anything, but their marriage was in trouble. Rachelle even mentioned the word divorce to me. That was what the trip was supposed to be about, working on their marriage. They hadn't had a chance to spend much time together this last year or so, what with Rachelle's shooting schedule and Alex's work. It was kind of a second honeymoon, I guess, and I got the feeling it was also kind of a last chance for the marriage."

I thought this was beginning to go on too long. "What made the police decide to call this a homicide?"

She glanced at me as though wondering what gave me the right to ask questions, but Miles's silence seemed to be waiting for an answer as well. She looked at him as she spoke. "They found some piece of equipment—a regulator, I think, I don't know, I'm not a diver. But they found this piece of equipment lodged in a crevice in one of the caves a couple of hundred yards from where Alex said they were diving, and they claim it had been tampered with. Then some boater, miles away from the dive site, said he saw a man toss something overboard that night that was big enough to be a body, and he insists the man was wearing a dive suit. It's ridiculous evidence, it doesn't even make sense, but we're not in the US and I guess it doesn't have to make sense. The police questioned Alex until two in the morning last night, and his lawyer thinks..." She drew another breath. "His lawyer thinks he could be arrested before the end of the week. Alex refuses to take any of it seriously, he insists it will all be straightened out any minute now... classic denial. But the authorities are holding his passport, and, Miles, if he's arrested, the lawyer says his bond will be at least half a million dollars...if he's allowed bond at all, which isn't at all certain." She looked at Miles helplessly. "I don't have that kind of money, and I don't know anyone here but you."

It was a good thing I had just taken a rather large bite of my crepe because I'm sure I would have said something I would regret otherwise. As it was, Rita and I exchanged a look that suggested she, too, was biting her tongue.

But, as he himself had so often pointed out, Miles was no fool. He said, with an air of easy authority that made me wonder how he knew such things, "If he knows there's a pending arrest, Alex should put the bond money in a revocable trust and assign a power of attorney. His lawyer should be able to handle the whole thing from here."

She was shaking her head before he finished speaking. "That's the problem. His business... well, from what I understand it hasn't been liquid for years. Rachelle was pouring money into it, but it wasn't making much of a difference. Alex is all but broke."

At this point, I literally had to bite the side of my tongue to keep from blurting what I was thinking. Rich wife, broke husband, fatal accident, missing body. Open and shut.

Rita murmured, "Oh, my."

Not exactly what I was thinking, but close enough.

A small frown appeared between Miles's brows, but otherwise he seemed calm. "So Rachelle had money?"

Susan looked incredulous. "You know who she was, don't you? The Denison-North entertainment dynasty? Oh, for heaven's sake, Miles, if it's not on the stock exchange it doesn't exist for you." There was an indulgent affection in her tone as she went on, "Her grandfather practically started television, he all but owned every network back when there were only three. Her father was Richard Denison, who wrote and produced thirty-six hit shows, and her mother is Alexia North, the movie star who died in that plane crash in the nineties…"

Rita murmured, "*That* Rachelle Denison. Good heavens."

Even I was impressed. Susan had not exaggerated when she used the word "dynasty", although "empire" or even "kingdom" might have been even more appropriate. We all should have made the connection sooner, but who would have guessed that someone with the last name "Denison" would turn out to be a third-rate actress in a canceled werewolf show?

Miles gave an impatient wave of his hand, and she went on, "Anyway, I suppose you could say she has money, if you consider being worth billions having money. She didn't come into full control of her trust until she was thirty, but the income from it alone was more than most people will see in a lifetime. The problem is that upon her death, the income ceases and of course Alex has no access to the trust. There's no way he can raise half a million dollars for bond, Miles."

And there went motive. If Rachelle's death cut off Alex Barry's only source of income, he had no reason to kill her. The question was, why didn't the police see that?

Or maybe they did, and had decided for whatever reason that motive didn't matter. I had been around law enforcement for too long to be under the delusion that the decisions that were made about such things were always rational. In fact, they were often the opposite.

As I had recently come to understand all too well.

Susan looked at Miles, her expression helpless. "Miles, I hate to ask, but I'm desperate. If it comes to that, if he is arrested, is there any way you could…?"

I watched in patent incredulity as Miles laid a reassuring hand atop hers on the table. "I'll look into it," he said. "And I'll try to get by to see Alex sometime today or tomorrow. Meantime, don't worry, okay?"

I saw her body visibly sag with relief, and a flash of tears brightened her eyes. Something about the way her nose went red as she fought back those tears made me not hate her as much as I wanted to. She stood up quickly, looking embarrassed. Miles stood as well. "Thank you," she said huskily. "I'll let you get back to your breakfast. It's good to see you again, Rita. Nice meeting you, Raine."

At least she got my name right.

"I'll see myself out," she told Miles, as he started to escort her to the front. "Please, I've taken enough of your day. Your daughter is adorable, Miles and…it was good seeing you."

She left quickly, heels clicking sharply on the wood deck.

To say the silence that followed her exit was awkward would have been a profound understatement. Fortunately it did not last very long.

"Well," said Rita brightly, standing. "I'll take care of some of these dishes."

I sprang to my feet, my voice as tight as my muscles. "I'll help."

Miles caught the hem of my tee shirt as I started to move past him. I glared at him, but he didn't let go. "The cleaning staff will take care of that," he said. And to his mother he added, "But maybe you could make sure Melanie is ready to go. Be sure she brings a pair of deck shoes."

Rita gave me a smile that was both sympathetic and reassuring, and hurried off. My eyes were churning cold fire as I looked at Miles. "Seriously?" I demanded. "You really want to do this now?"

"Not while you're looming over me like you're looking for a weapon," he replied. "Sit down."

I grasped the material of my tee shirt and jerked it out of his fingers. I sat down stiffly, my voice low, my fists clenched. "You lied to me. I asked you point-blank who Susan was and you lied. What was the point, Miles? Why did you even bother?

Or did you just do it for fun, just to see how foolish you could make me look? Well, I certainly hope it all lived up to your expectations because I've got to tell you, I thought it was hilarious."

He refilled his coffee cup, glancing at me. "Are you finished?"

"No, I'm not finished. And it's not as though you didn't have plenty of chances. We hadn't been here fifteen minutes when the driver mentioned Alex Barry and all you said was that you knew him. You couldn't have mentioned he was your brother-in-law? You didn't think that was something that might interest me?"

"Ex brother-in-law," he pointed out.

My fists tightened in my lap. "This was a bad idea. I never should have come here. I told you that. I knew I wouldn't have a good time. This is your world, not mine. These are your friends, your exes, your expensive French food and designer sunglasses and business associates who throw bodies off yachts, for God's sake. I don't belong here."

"Okay," Miles said, "now you're finished." He sipped his coffee, his gaze cool. "These are not my friends, they're people I know. One of them I happened to be married to for eight months twelve years ago and haven't seen more than half a dozen times since. As for what my business associates—

or former in-laws— may or may not have done
regarding crimes against persons...are you sure you
want to go there?"

He was right, I didn't want to go there. In the
brief time I had known him I had been involved
with more crimes and criminals than he probably
had in his entire life, and even though an argument
certainly could be made that none of it was my
fault, that was not an argument I wanted to have.

He went on, "And if you want to know why I
didn't tell you Susan was my ex-wife, this is why.
Because I knew you'd do this. Because I wanted
you to have a few days when you didn't have to be
angry at anyone, or worried about anything, and
because there's no reason for you to do either one. I
didn't lie to you. I just didn't tell you what you
didn't need to know."

"You lied to me!" I hissed back. "You lied to
me by not telling the whole truth and hoping you
wouldn't get caught, just like—"

I was going to say "just like my father, just like
my ex husband, just like every man I've ever
known!" but I stopped myself, shocked and a little
horrified at what had almost come spilling out. But
I could see by the quiet, all-too-knowing look in
Miles's eyes and by the slight tightening of the
corners of his lips that I might as well have gone

ahead and said it. I had convicted myself with my own unspoken truth.

He said, "I don't make a lot of promises any more. After three divorces it seems little pointless. But the ones I do make these days I make sure I can keep. I told you once I'm not going to give up on you just because you keep trying to see if I will. That's a promise. Here's another one." He sipped his coffee, his expression neutral, his tone matter of fact. "I'm done paying for the mistakes other men have made. I'm not your father. I'm not your ex-husband. I'm not your college boyfriend who told you he loved you and then set you up to take the rap for a felony. Those guys deserve your anger, and worse. I don't. So work out your issues. Get therapy if you need it. I'm here to listen, to help where I can, and to try to make sure nobody ever hurts you like that again. But I'm not going to take the beating for something I didn't do. That's a promise." He put down his coffee cup, and invited in the same mild, even tone, "Something you'd like to say to me now? I'd be particularly interested in anything that begins with, 'I'm sorry, Miles, I should have given you a chance to explain.'"

He was the one whose ex-wife had just waltzed up to the breakfast table unannounced and asked him for a half million dollars and somehow it was all my fault. He was the one who had failed to even mention that his ex-wife was on the island in the first place, much less that her brother might be involved in a murder, and *I* was supposed to apologize? The man had told me to get therapy, for heaven's sake. Oh, I had lots to say.

Except that he'd been right. Not about the therapy, but about my blaming him for things that weren't his fault. That was the essence of my relationship with Miles: I never knew whether I wanted to strangle him or fling myself into his arms and let him hold me until everything that was wrong was somehow right again, which he always managed to do. He hadn't lied; he had just been trying to protect me. And the infuriating thing was that he thought that made it okay.

Just like my father. Damn it. *Damn it.*

I swallowed a lump in my throat, and with it all the words that suddenly didn't need to be said after all. I said, a little gruffly, "I forgive you."

He almost smiled. "Thank you."

"But I don't need therapy."

He responded with only a slight quirk of his eyebrow. "Okay."

I hesitated. "Are you going to give her the money?"

"Him," he corrected. "The money would be for Alex." And a small thoughtful frown shadowed his eyes as he answered, "I don't know yet."

I flung open my hands in exasperation. "Now *that* I don't understand. You think he's guilty—"

He lifted a finger in objection. "I didn't say that. I said he's capable of being guilty."

"Then why would you put up your own money to keep him out of jail?"

"Did you ever hear that old saying, 'Keep your friends close and your enemies closer?' Besides…" the thoughtful expression was back again, "I don't think he's going to jail. He's too smart for that."

I took a deep breath. "What you did wasn't right, Miles. This…" I struggled briefly for the words, "this thing between us can't go any further if you keep secrets. Don't shut me out."

"I won't."

And that, in the end, was all I had ever really wanted.

I released a breath of satisfaction and got to my feet. "So," I said, doing my best to summon enthusiasm for the day ahead, "are we going snorkeling, or what?

The morning that followed was demonstrable proof of why it doesn't pay to hold a grudge. Rita elected to stay at home, claiming she preferred to do her swimming in a pool and didn't trust any ocean-going vessel that was too small to accommodate a casino. I had quickly grown to enjoy her company and I was sorry she wouldn't be spending the day on the water with us, particularly since Miles was still on shaky ground with me... and perhaps vice-versa. It wouldn't have hurt to have an extra buffer between us, just to make sure the conversation stayed civilized.

As soon as I saw the marina, though, any secret lingering annoyance I might have felt was pushed aside and swallowed up by much more immediate distractions. Like Cisco, I hardly knew which way to look, there were so many intriguing sights and smells and sounds. The dock was lined with dozens, perhaps hundreds, of brilliantly white boats gently bobbing on the crystal water: small boats, large boats, sail-boats, motor- boats, party boats and house-boats—which, in this environment, were more accurately known as yachts. Cisco's head swiveled toward a Yorkie that ran to the rail of a mid-sized sail boat, barking madly as we passed, and then toward a sheltie, its immaculately groomed coat shining in the sun, who joined the chorus a few boats down. Somewhere a bigger dog—perhaps a lab or a golden—barked back from inside a cabin. I was beginning to understand why Miles hadn't hesitated about inviting all my dogs to come along; this place was a canine playground. It was all I could do to keep Cisco in a semi-heel as we made our way down the dock, and my focus wasn't much better than his. I tore my gaze from a party boat filled with what I was sure were French models sunning themselves on the deck, to a gaggle of paparazzi gathered around another hoping for a shot of whatever celebrity was onboard, to a rock band that was setting up on the deck of another yacht, to a labradoodle that was racing wildly from one vantage point to the other on the deck of his boat, barking and trying to get a better look at Cisco who, like his mistress, was trying to take it all in at once. This mountain girl was definitely not in Kansas anymore. So to speak.

Miles's boat was a medium-sized sail boat with what he called a "shallow draw", which meant it could easily navigate around the sandbars and reefs as well as the deeper waters where he liked to dive. And since neither Melanie nor I was a very good crew, it was a good thing he could maneuver the boat without any help. He took us out a few hundred yards from shore and anchored near a reef where the turquoise water was so clear you could actually see the fish from the deck. However, when we put on our snorkeling masks and swam in the midst of schools of darting silver, gold, green and blue sea life it was like nothing I'd ever seen or experienced. Cisco stayed in the boat for the first part of the trip, leaning over the rail with his ears flopping forward while his eyes eagerly followed the flashes of fish movement, barking now and then just to see the fish scatter.

When I could feel my shoulders start to burn, I took a break from the water and, at Melanie's insistence, released Cisco to paddle around the boat with her. Since we were in barely four feet of water and there were other small boats nearby, I wasn't concerned about either of them, and apparently Miles felt the same because after a time he joined me on deck, and we watched the two merry-makers in the water below us while he rubbed sunscreen on my back. I settled back in   the shade of the awning over the helm, and he sat out on a towel in the sun.

I glanced around at the other small boats swaying in the water around us, some of them close enough that I could hear voices. I said, "I don't suppose we're anywhere near the place where Rachelle Denison disappeared."

"The other side of the island." Miles settled a baseball cap on his head and put on his sunglasses. His bronze shoulders, still damp with sea water, gleamed in the sunlight. I was glad we weren't fighting anymore.

"But if it's a popular dive site, it's probably just as crowded as this one."

"Usually." He leaned back on his elbows and turned his face to the sun.

"Miles, how do you suppose that regulator got wedged in a crevice?"

"Anything can happen underwater."

I lifted my sunglasses to give him a meaningful look, but succeeded only in blinding myself with the bright sun. I let them drop to the bridge of my nose again. "You're not being very helpful."

"I'm on vacation."

"Will you teach me to dive?"

"Not this trip."

I confess, I liked the fact that he thought there might be other trips.

"Why not?"

He sat up, gazing over the side of the boat to look for Melanie, who had put her snorkel mask back on and was snapping pictures with her underwater camera. He needn't have worried; I was watching her, as well as Cisco who treaded water beside her. "Because," he said, "I have a feeling the main thing you want to know about diving is what a regulator is and how it could be tampered with."

Melanie surfaced and took of her mask, laughing. "Great pictures, Dad! The fish are swimming around Cisco's feet!"

"You'll have to submit them to *Underwater* Magazine," he called back to her. "Bet you win a prize."

"Cool!" She put her mask back on and ducked under the water again.

Miles retrieved his phone from the bench storage compartment where he had left it, and began to scroll through his messages. I watched Cisco for signs of fatigue, but, like his human counterpart, he seemed to be having too much fun, snapping at the water and playing tag with Melanie, to get tired. I decided to give him a few more minutes.

I turned to Miles. "So?"

"So what?

"What is a regulator and how can it be tampered with?"

"The regulator controls the pressure of the air divers breathe." He didn't glance up, at least as far as I could tell. "When people talk about the regulator they're usually referring to the mouthpiece they see the diver breathing through, but it has lots of parts. You want the whole run-down or the condensed version?"

"Condensed is fine for now."

"So that's it. It's basically a pressure gauge attached to hoses. As for what can go wrong, almost anything. Turn the wrong valve and the whole tank can bleed dry in a matter of seconds."

"Causing you to depend on your dive partner to share his oxygen."

"Which is not a problem if your buddy has an octopus—a spare regulator—otherwise it can be dicey. Panic can hit anybody in an out-of-air situation, and if they refuse to return the regulator..."

"Then you would have to do what you can to save yourself."

"Right."

"Do you have one of those spare regulators on your equipment?"

"Sure. Most experienced divers do."

"I wonder why Alex Barry didn't."

"Good question."

"Why don't you ask him?"

"Because I'm on vacation."

I gazed meaningfully at the phone. "So what exactly constitutes a vacation for you, Miles?"

He finished the text he was sending and turned off the phone, then leaned across and gave me a quick kiss. "We're having drinks with Alex Barry this afternoon. Happy?"

I was also surprised. "We are?"

"You told me not to shut you out."

I couldn't help smiling. That was another thing I liked about Miles. He was a fast learner.

❀ ❦ ❀ ❦ ❀ ❦

CHAPTER SIX

We met at a place called The Harbor Club, which was reached via a shell drive lined with dolphin topiaries. There was a golf course-like lawn with a giant fountain and reflecting pool, and flower beds brilliant with red and yellow and bright pink blooms. The interior was a surprising contrast— lots of dark wood and ships' wheels, deep green leather club chairs drawn up in intimate circles around polished mahogany tables. The floor to ceiling window in front of which we were sitting was shaped like a ship's prow and had a magnificent view of the bay and the marina crowded with boats, but even it was coated with sun-darkening film so that we could see out but no one could see in.

Alex Barry was a slender, gray-haired man with pale features and a small precise mouth that somehow gave him an air of distinction while at the same time making me not want to trust him. He had already claimed a table and he stood when we approached. His smile was pleasant but the way his faded denim eyes flicked over me, head to toe, reminded me of a snake's tongue, and I took an unconscious step closer to Miles. I was actually glad to feel the possessive touch of his hand on my back. Already I knew why Miles didn't like him. The word sleazy came to mind.

Miles introduced us and Alex immediately ordered a round of drinks—a white wine for me, a refill of the scotch he'd been drinking, and, without asking, a club soda for Miles. So he knew him that well. But, I supposed, having once been his brother-in-law, he would. He settled back in the deep club chair, adjusting his jacket, and smiled.

"So, Miles, still tea-totaling, I see," he said. "One day that's going to catch up with you, you know."

"I'll take my chances," returned Miles pleasantly. He added soberly. "I'm sorry about Rachelle."

Alex nodded, and for a moment he looked like what he was supposed to be—grieving, and in shock. He said thickly, "I am too." He finished off his drink and met Miles's gaze. "Susan told me she talked to you."

"That's why I'm here," replied Miles in a tone that was as even and direct as Alex's. I liked the way these men did business, even if it was a little intimidating. And even if this wasn't exactly business.

As though reading my mind, Alex flashed me a quick, tight smile. "But no need to go into that right now when there's a lovely lady at the table. That would not only be rude, it would be a crime against nature, wouldn't you agree?" Without waiting for a response, he turned to me. "What do you do, Raine?"

"I'm a dog trainer," I told him. I wondered if he had ever met one of those before. I suspected that when other men, including Miles, introduced their girlfriends to Alex Barry, the names were generally followed by the word "model", "actress" , "lawyer" or maybe even "CEO". Not dog trainer.

"Are you?" If he was surprised he didn't show it, which was a point for him, I guessed. He picked up his glass again, realized it was empty, and set it down. "You should meet the fellow who works for me, Rick Chambliss. Great with dogs. That's why I put him in charge of setting up for all our clients who have dogs." He glanced around impatiently for the waitress.

"I think I've met him, actually," I said. "He was on the beach with Cocoa."

"Right." A small frown. "That crazy dog. He never was good for anyone but Rachelle. She had him trained to the camera, did you know that? You never saw a picture of her without that dog, it was like her trademark. But when she wasn't around, he was wild, completely out of control. I don't know what I'm going to do with him now."

"Did you find him, yet?" I asked. "Your sister said he ran away."

"No, not yet." His smile was faintly self-deprecating, vaguely wry. "You're the expert, Raine. Do you think he knew Rachelle wasn't coming back? Do you think he just decided there was no point in hanging around anymore?"

"I think dogs know when something's wrong in their household," I told him. "They've survived for thousands of years by learning to read human moods, behavior and body language better than any other animal on the planet. And they're very dependent on routine. When their routine is disrupted it can be stressful. And some dogs react to stress by running. It's instinct, really. They respond to pain by trying to run from it."

Alex murmured, "Don't we all?"

The waitress arrived then with our drinks, but I couldn't help noting he did not ask whether I thought Cocoa might come back. That was usually the first thing people asked about a missing dog, mostly because they needed someone to reassure them that yes, the chances were good that they would see their beloved pet again. But of course Alex had made it clear Cocoa was not *his* beloved pet.

Even though I knew Miles had more important things to talk about, I was confused about something. I asked Alex, "I thought Rick was just your dog walker. What did you mean when you said he set up for your clients with dogs?"

Miles answered that one. "Alex's company runs the concierge service," he said. "I thought I mentioned that."

"I bought it a couple of years ago," Alex explained, "and made it part of the security package. It makes things easier for the people who have part-time homes here to have one company in charge of everything from maid service to fire and theft protection. "

So Rick had been the one who set up Cisco's bed and dog dishes. I'd have to thank him, if I saw him again.

Miles said, "Susan said business hasn't been going all that well."

He blew out a dismissive breath and waved away the notion as though it were a pesky fly. But the nervous darting of his eyes gave him away. "What does she know? I don't see her more than once or twice a year and all of a sudden she's the expert on everything. Hard to lose money in the security business in a down economy, old son, you know that. Crime goes up, so do my contracts. Hard to lose money."

"Yet somehow you managed it," Miles said.

There was a flash of something as hard as a knife blade in his eyes, but it was just a flash. And the cool, confident smile that played around the edges of his lips remained in place. "Is that a fact?"

Miles said, "You've got two lawsuits pending in Colorado that you are not going to win. You lost the Crichton Contracting account last year when one of your employees was arrested for stealing from a construction site. Turns out he had a criminal record that you didn't disclose."

"We use ex-cons a good deal in this business," replied Alex, unperturbed. "Who knows security better than the people who've made a career out of getting around it? Of course, you realize I'm the one who turned him in."

"About two minutes before the police were about to close in anyway," Miles went on. "But it didn't stop Crichton from pulling out. After that, new clients have been a little hard to come by, as far as I can tell. Not to mention that biotech investment that went sour last year, and the SEC case you spent five years and a couple of million trying to keep from going to court. Congratulations on that, by the way. Not many people even knew about it."

The eyes got harder, the smile didn't waver. "You had me investigated, Miles? And you're not even a stockholder."

"For which I'm feeling pretty grateful right now." He leaned back, took a sip of his club soda, and put the glass down. "You've done a good job for me over the years, Alex. You've probably done a good job for most of your clients. But you've had a run of bad luck. Your business is circling the drain. Did you marry Rachelle for her money?"

I glanced at Miles, impressed. And here I had been thinking I was going to have to figure out a way to ask the hard questions. I settled back and sipped my wine, enjoying the show.

Alex looked annoyed. "Of course not. That's a completely inappropriate question. Besides..." he glanced at me, trying to replace the annoyance in his expression with politeness, and achieving nothing more than a smirk, "we're boring your lady friend."

Miles glanced at me. "Are you bored, sugar?"

"Not at all," I assured him. "In fact, I'm fascinated. Please go on."

Miles said, "I tell Raine everything. I like her to know who my associates are."

I turned a killer look on him, but of course Alex Barry could have no way of knowing how tongue in cheek that was.

"Raine has some experience in criminal investigation," Miles went on, his tone a bit more sincere now. "I thought she might be able to help us unravel how things stand in this police investigation."

I managed to keep the surprise out of my face, and just sipped my wine complacently when Alex looked at me. After all, it was true. I did have experience…after a fashion.

Alex smiled thinly at me. "Is that right? Maybe you should come work for me."

"Thanks," I said. "I have a job." And before he could make further inquiries into my experience, I said, "I know this must be hard for you. Do you have any idea why the police suspect you?" Sometimes a woman's touch is required.

He gave a terse shake of his head. "Because they have to suspect someone and I was the only one there. Because the press is starting to turn this into a circus. Because of who I am, and who she was. I don't know. The whole thing is insane. It was an accident. Anyone can see that."

Of course he had left out the most important "because". Because they couldn't find the body. If there had been a body, it might have been much easier to determine whether or not an accident had been the cause of death.

Miles said, "Why don't you tell us what happened?"

Alex Barry looked at him steadily. "I didn't kill her, Miles." It was perhaps the first time since we'd sat down that his eyes had not darted or shifted at least once. That made his statement slightly more convincing.

"That might not matter if you're arrested here," Miles said. "We both know the problems that can crop up when international law is involved."

"You're probably tired of telling the story," I offered sympathetically. "If it's too hard for you, I understand." Again, the woman's touch.

Alex looked at me for a moment as though he wasn't quite sure whether to trust me, which was, I was sure, a look he gave a lot of people. And apparently my woman's touch was not quite as effective as I had hoped because he said flatly, "As a matter of fact, I am tired of talking about it."

Miles coaxed, "Do it anyway."

He gave him a steely eyed glare for just a moment, tossed back some scotch, and then said, "Rachelle wanted to celebrate ourt anniversary on the island. She had a big party planned and everything. We always take the boat out to the reef our first night here, it's like a tradition, a big thing with her. We take a picnic and dive the reef, always the same."

"Because that's where you proposed to her," I guessed.

He looked surprised, and then nodded. "To tell the truth I wasn't that much into it that night. Somebody had sent her a bottle of champagne to celebrate this new part she'd gotten, and I don't know, maybe she had too much of it. She was acting a little odd."

"Odd how?"

He shrugged. "I don't know. Hyper. Goofy. I remember asking her if she was good to dive, but then she seemed to get it together and acted okay until we got in the water. We'd only been down about ten minutes when she signaled she was almost out of air. I thought it was her gauge, but we started back anyway."

"Didn't she check her gear before she went in?" Miles asked.

"We both did, before we loaded it on the boat that afternoon. The police say the hose on the regulator they found had been sliced, but I don't see how she could have missed a thing like that in broad daylight."

"Why do you suppose they only found that one piece of equipment in the cave?" I asked. "Shouldn't it have been, well, you know, with the rest of the equipment?"

"The theory is that in her panic she took off her gear and tried to swim to the surface without it. The currents around the caves can get strong enough to break it apart. Or..." and his eyes met mine. "someone planted it there. All I know is that if they'd been able to prove that it belonged to Rachelle, I'd probably be in jail right now. "

"New moon," Miles murmured thoughtfully.

"Right. Rachelle never used a dive light when we were together. She claimed that both of our lights in the water made it too bright. And we anchored far enough away from the reef that the lights wouldn't disturb the marine life."

I was confused, and my expression must have shown it. "Usually with a night dive your only light is your dive light," Miles explained, "and whatever ambient light is on the surface. That's the whole point. On a dark night, with no shore lights or boat lights, and only one dive light, it would be hard to notice the excess bubbles if you were using air at a faster rate than normal. Or if there was a leak."

"Right," said Alex briefly. "And I didn't." He took another drink of scotch. "At forty feet she started panicking, grabbing at my regulator. She was completely out of air. I started buddy breathing, but she was in full-blown panic, sucking air like a freight train, and when it was time to give the regulator back, she wouldn't. I finally got it back from her, but in the struggle I think she got disoriented. She pushed off and started swimming the other way. I tried to go after her, but the currents were stirring up a lot of silt. I couldn't see her, I was running low on air, I had to surface."

Miles said, "Did you search the caves?"

"Not then. When I got to the boat, I ditched my gear and did a shallow dive with my light, hoping she'd seen the boat light and was swimming toward me." He gave another brief shake of his head. "Of course, time was out. I must have known that, but you have to try. I went back up and sounded the claxon for help. I got new tanks and went back down. There were a couple of other boats out that night, eventually somebody came. But we never found her."

Miles's face was very somber, and I knew that, as someone who had actually been beneath the water, he was living the horror of that night in his mind. I mentally retracted whatever wish I might have expressed to learn to scuba dive. And I literally could not imagine the desperation of the moment when a man had to choose to leave his wife behind or die.

Miles said, "Why did you only have one regulator?"

"I sent my equipment in for repair when I was down last month. Hadn't had a chance to pick it up. I was using a spare." He was quiet for a moment. "She was a good diver. That was the one thing we had in common. You never expect something like this to happen. I still don't understand how it did. Was it my fault she died? I don't know. Maybe there was something I could have done. But I know I didn't kill her."

Miles said, "Did the police ask about life insurance?"

Alex gave him a look that was half admiring, half resentful. "They did. And they were disappointed. Her policy contained a hazardous activities exclusion. So does mine. Scuba diving, as you know, is a named hazardous activity. The policy won't pay a cent."

And there went the last possible motive. Unless...

Miles had the same thought, but asked the question with a good deal less tact that I would have. I was beginning to see the advantage of having him around. He said, "Did Rachelle ask you for a divorce?"

Alex looked so startled I couldn't believe he was acting. "What? Who told you that?"

I glanced at Miles. "Your sister mentioned it. She said they had lunch before she left to come here."

Alex frowned a little. "Really? Why would they do that?"

I said, "I thought they were close."

"Were they?" He shrugged. "Maybe. I guess they might have worked together once or twice. I think Susan introduced her to some people—her understudy, I think, and maybe a director." Something must have shown on my face, or Miles's, because he added defensively, "Okay, so I didn't keep up with every little detail of her life. But the girl was crazy about me. This whole trip was her idea. Jeez, that's all I need, for the press to get hold of a rumor about divorce."

Because if it could be proven that Rachelle had been about to divorce him, taking all of her money plus half of his business, that might be a motive for murder. Maybe.

I said, "Speaking of the press, aren't you worried that coming out like this for drinks only a couple of days after your wife died will make you look bad?" I could remember more than one case where a spouse, or even the parent of a missing child, had been convicted by the press long before trial simply because he or she had failed to grieve properly.

He darted a hard glance at me. "No," he said flatly. "I'm a free man. And an innocent one. I'll do what I damn well please."

He was *so* going down. For a moment I actually felt a little sorry for him.

"That's why," he went on, and tossed back the last of his scotch, "I've decided to beat the blood-sucking bastards at their own game. I've called a press conference for exactly…" he glanced at his watch, "fifteen minutes from now on the harbor side deck to clear this thing up once and for all. I won't be held hostage in my own home, and I refuse to live my life under a cloud of speculation. I can't stop people from making up their own stories, but I can at least get the truth out there." He smiled thinly. "You're welcome to attend, of course. In fact, you might have saved yourself some time by skipping the drinks and watching it on television."

"Gutsy move," Miles said .

"Actually, it was Susan's idea," he said. He glanced at his glass as though hoping it might magically refill itself. "I guess she's good for something."

There was a slight tightening of the corners of his lips, but Miles said nothing. His silence was more condemning than any words could have been, as I had had the opportunity to discover on more than one occasion. And it didn't take Alex more than a few seconds to catch on.

"All right," he said brusquely. "I know she asked you stand bail for me. It was her idea, not mine. You got what you came for, I told you everything I know. Do it, don't do it. I've got plenty of other friends." He waved the waitress over. "I have to get out there. We'll have a game of golf next time I'm out your way. Put this on my tab, sweetheart," he told the waitress, then looked at me as he stood. "Nice to meet you, Raine. You seem like a sweet girl. Probably too good for this SOB." The way he said it was supposed to be joking, but there was absolutely no mirth in his eyes. "Take care." He nodded to Miles. "Miles."

I watched him cross the room with a mixture of astonishment and distaste. I looked back at Miles. "I feel like I need a shower," I said.

"You and me, too, sweetheart." The fact that he made no attempt to turn that into a double entendre only proved how distracted he was. "So, what did you think?"

"Oh, I think he's going to jail," I assured him, "as soon as the police can scrape together some kind of motive."

"I think so, too. I'm also going to offer bail."

I stared at him. "What?"

"Relax. There's no way in hell a judge is going to set bail, and this way I get to look like a hero."

To whom? I wondered. Alex, or Susan?

"But first," Miles added, "I'm going to start looking for a new security company. It's just a little too much of a coincidence to me that there've been over two dozen break-ins in the past two years in properties that he manages. Either he's not very good at what he does or—"

"He's not screening those ex-con employees of his very well," I supplied thoughtfully.

"That one's got my vote. Either way, now that he's in the spotlight it won't be long before other big clients start noticing the coincidence, if they haven't already. I give that company six months."

"So even if he doesn't go to jail, he's screwed."

"Barring a huge influx of cash and a few years to rebuild, yes. Want to go to the press conference, or have you had enough?"

I thought about it for only a moment. "I've had enough *and* I want to go."

His expression was wry. "Not that I'm surprised, but do you mind if I ask why?"

"I'm protecting your investment. If Mr. Barry by any chance manages to come off as more sincere in his public statement than he did to us, he might actually get bail. In which case you might want to reconsider your ambitions to be a hero."

He regarded me with a touch of amused resignation in his eyes and a small shake of his head. "Well, at least you had twenty-four hours of vacation." He laid a bill on the table and stood up, extending his hand to me. "Shall we go?"

So much, I supposed, for my vow to be normal for a week. I felt a little bad about that, and as we left the building for the brilliant sunshine of the wide deck that encircled the building, I slipped my arm around Miles's waist and gave him a squeeze, pressing my head against his shoulder. "That was hot, by the way," I said.

He lifted a quizzical eyebrow, pulling out his sunglasses. "The way I over-tipped?"

"The way you interrogated the suspect. I didn't know you had it in you."

"In my line of work it's called 'reading the table'. And you'd be amazed at the things I have in me."

"So I'm beginning to suspect."

As we came around the corner we found the deck blocked off by orange cones, beyond which black electrical cords snaked toward a lectern upon which several microphones had been mounted. I recognized the logos of a couple of US entertainment news organizations on those microphones, and the green lawn below the deck was populated with almost a dozen reporters and camera men.

"Rachelle Denison must have been more famous than I realized," I murmured as we went down the steps toward the lawn. "There are a lot of reporters from the States."

"If you were a reporter in Arkansas or Detroit with a chance to cover a story in St. Bart's, would you turn it down?"

"Good point."

We found a place at the edge of the collection of reporters, but close to the deck. I could see Alex Barry, looking appropriately somber, talking quietly to his sister. I don't know why I was surprised to find her there. She was wearing a simple summer suit with her hair pulled back, and in contrast to the distress she had displayed this morning, she looked calm and in control. Looking up, she noticed Miles, and her face softened a little as she acknowledged him. He nodded back to her. There was nothing more to it than that, but it made me uneasy. There were other people on the deck with them, one of whom Miles identified as Jeff Lennox, an attorney, and a couple of others who, from their stance on either side of the door, I suspected were security guards. And standing somewhat to the side, not a part of Alex's entourage but clearly interested in it, was a small neat man in a suit that I immediately identified as a policeman. I have an instinct for them.

Alex Barry glanced at his watch, stepped to the lectern, leaned forward into the microphone bank, and said, "Thank you all for coming. I'm Alex Barry. I'd like to make a brief statement, and then I'll take your questions. I want to be as forthcoming with you as I can, so I'll tell you everything I know. And thank you in advance for your patience and understanding during this very difficult time."

He was a completely different man than the one who had so cavalierly tossed back scotch while relating his story only a few moments ago. I glanced at Miles and saw one corner of his lips curve faintly upward in contempt.

Alex went on, "On Friday night, my wife went for a dive off the Pain du Sucre reef. It was one of our favorite places, and we dived it many times before. Rachelle was an excellent diver, and the reef is considered safe for all divers. For reasons we haven't yet determined, Rachelle used up the air in her tanks sooner than anticipated, and we were forced to surface early. Even though I tried to share my tanks with her, she became disoriented and panicky, and started swimming away from the boat. I tried to rescue her but had to surface when I, too, ran low on air." A dramatic pause, and then he continued in a broken voice. "I never saw Rachelle again."

A murmur and shuffle went through the crowd on the lawn as reporters began to formulate their questions, but Alex's attention was distracted by a stirring behind him. The glass doors from the Harbor Club opened and he turned, a flicker of outrage crossing his face at the indignity of the intrusion. Susan turned as well, staring, and her hand fluttered to her throat.

Someone beside me said, "Holy crap."

A woman in a big white hat and sunglasses wearing a white gauzy sundress walked out onto the deck. I was close enough to hear her say to an astonished Alex, "Until now, darling."

She had a thick mane of rich auburn hair, which fell loose around her shoulders as she took off her hat. She walked deliberately to the lectern and stood beside Alex. She removed her sunglasses. A gasp went through the crowd.

She stood there for a moment, letting them all get a good look, and then she leaned toward the crowd. Her voice was low and rich, her smile strained and apologetic. "Ladies and gentlemen," she said, "I am so terribly sorry for all the fuss. But as you can plainly see, and at the risk of sounding like a dreadful cliché—I'm afraid the rumors of my death have been greatly exaggerated."

"Jesus and Mary," breathed the reporter next to me. "That's Rachelle Denison."

CHAPTER SEVEN

The crowd erupted around us. "Miss Denison!" " Miss Denison!" "What happened out there?" "Where have you been the past forty-eight hours?" "Was this all part of the publicity for your new film?" "Miss Denison! "

They surged toward the deck, cameras clicking, wires trailing, everyone shouting at once. It was hard to know where to look. The two men I'd assumed to be security guards proved my assumption correct by rushing in front of Rachelle Denison and spreading their arms to keep the crowd at bay. She sounded a little frantic as she said into the microphone, "Please, please I'll answer your questions if you'll just give me a moment!" The lawyer stepped up and said something into her ear.

And Alex Barry just stood there, white faced, staring.

Susan came forward and I lost sight of what was going on for a minute while someone pushed in front of me and lifted a camera high overhead. When I was able to see again, the two security guards were hurrying Rachelle toward the glass doors behind them, and the lawyer had hold of Alex's arm, urging him to follow. Susan stood in front of the podium, holding up her hands for quiet. She didn't get it.

"Please!" Susan called. "Please!"

"Miss Denison!"

"Turn this way!'

"One more shot!"

"Do you know what happened?"

"Did you expect this? What is your reaction?"

Susan said loudly, "Gentlemen! Ladies! This is a shock for the family, as I'm sure you can appreciate. Please give us a moment. I promise we'll have something for you as soon as we can."

Somebody shouted, "My deadline is five o'clock!"

Someone else demanded, "Who are you?"

Susan, wisely in my opinion, chose to make her escape and turned to follow her brother through the glass doors. The other man, the one I had guessed to be a policeman, followed.

Miles turned to me. "Well," he said with a shrug, "I guess that's that. Shall we go?"

I could see my reflection in his sunglasses, and the astonishment on my face would have been comical in other circumstances. My jaw actually dropped. "Are you *kidding*?"

"Yes." He put his arm around my shoulders and swept me through the crowd, up the steps, and through the glass door just before it closed behind the policeman. "Friend of the family," he identified himself briefly when it looked as though the policeman might object, and jerked off his sunglasses. "Susan, what the hell?"

We were in a small meeting room typical of such rooms everywhere—beige curtains and walls, a conference table with dark wooden chairs pushed up against a wall, a cart with AV equipment in a corner—and it was almost as chaotic in here as it had been outside. I pushed my sunglasses up into my hair and glanced around while Miles bore down on his ex-wife. Rachelle Denison, who, now that I saw her in person, did look vaguely familiar, was in intense conversation with the lawyer and her husband, all of them talking at once so that it was impossible to catch anything clearly. I heard words like. "Thought you were dead!" and "How can you"— and "If you'll just give me a chance—"

Susan's voice caught my attention. "Miles, I'm so glad you're here!" I turned that way in time to see her grasp Miles's hands in a way that seemed both desperate and intimate, and when she touched him the annoyance left his face. "I don't —can't believe this! Rachelle, oh my God, it's really you!"

Susan left Miles to push her way between her brother and the lawyer, and she grasped Rachelle by the shoulders, staring at her for just an instant. Then she whispered, "Oh my God!" and Rachelle started to cry the kind of tears that are mixed with joy and so did Susan, and they embraced. Maybe it was just me, but I thought it was a little odd her husband hadn't done the same thing the moment he saw her.

I murmured out loud, mostly to myself. "She certainly does look healthy for a woman who's supposed to have been dead for two days."

The policeman who stood beside me agreed, "My thoughts exactly, mademoiselle."

His French accent, though not particularly heavy, along with his pencil moustache and dapper appearance, reminded me of Inspector Poirot, which made me feel at ease with him immediately. He probably used that resemblance to his advantage a good deal, but then again how much major crime could there be on a resort island like this?

He asked my name, and I told him, and Miles's name too. He wrote both of them down. I added, "I'm just a guest here. I don't really know anyone involved. But in the States we have laws against people who file false police reports."

His smile was tight and brief. "We are a small island with an even smaller security force, mademoiselle, and greatly dependent in our economy on the goodwill of those who visit us here. It is for the most part in the best interest of all concerned to close this case on a happy note. Now, if you will forgive me, I shall now make an attempt to do just that."

He left me with a small bow, which I liked, and approached Rachelle and Susan, who were wiping each other's tears between exclamations of joy and relief. Alex was just staring at them with an expression on his face that we in the mountains called "poleaxed". I've never known exactly what that means, but I know what it looks like.

The policeman said, "Madame Denison, my name is Inspector LeClerk. May I express how relieved we all are to see you looking so well? The island of St. Barthelemy has devoted a great many resources over the past two days to the process of recovering your mortal remains from the depth of the ocean where, we were given to believe, your life had been lost. Perhaps you would do me the kindness of explaining how you come to be standing here today?"

Miles touched my shoulder, murmuring, "This I've got to hear."

Susan found some tissues; Rachelle dabbed at her eyes. The lawyer murmured something to her, and pulled out one of the chairs at the table for her. She sat down , and Susan took a chair beside her, holding her hand. Everyone else stood. I moved a little closer.

Rachelle took a breath, and balled the tissue in her free hand. She said, "I'm sorry. I know everyone's been worried. I…" There was a slight hitch in her voice, and she glanced down to compose herself. Susan squeezed her fingers bracingly, and Rachelle managed a faint smile when she looked up again. "I thought I was dead, too."

She took another breath. "It was my fault." She glanced apologetically at her husband. "I didn't tell Alex I was taking diet pills. I had to drop some weight for this new role, and I had to do it quickly. I shouldn't have had the champagne, but it was a tradition and…" She looked at him with big wet eyes. "I'm sorry, darling. I'm so sorry."

He remained impassive.

The inspector prompted, "So you went diving after mixing diet pills and champagne."

She nodded, looking ashamed. "It was stupid, but my judgment was impaired. I didn't realize how fast I was using up my air until it was almost gone. After that it's all a blur. I know Alex tried to help me but I was terrified, my heart was going like a freight train, I thought I was dying. I lost Alex. I didn't have a dive light. All I could think to do was to ditch my equipment and try to surface. But I didn't know where the surface was."

A long silence while she, presumably, relived that horrible night. This was the second time I had heard the story, though from vastly differently points of view, in a very short time, and the only thing I knew for certain was that it would take an act of God to ever get me in scuba equipment.

Finally the inspector said, "One presumes you did, eventually, find the surface."

She nodded, too emotional to speak.

"Why didn't you call for help? You could not have been far from the boat."

"I didn't see it at first. There was chop, and I was exhausted, all I could do was tread water and try to get my strength back. I heard the emergency claxon and I tried to call out for help. My voice was too weak, and the current kept pulling me farther and farther away from the boat. Eventually I had to swim with it just to stay alive. I swam until I saw the lights of shore, and I let the tide carry me in. The next thing I remember I woke up in a bed in this little beach cottage, with this French woman trying to get me to drink some juice, still wearing my dive suit... I think her husband had found me that morning on the beach but..." she smiled apologetically, "my French is not very good. I didn't realize how much time had passed, but I was terribly weak and dehydrated. I slept off and on for a long time. The better part of two days, I guess. "

It sounded like the plot to a movie. In fact, I think I had seen it.

Apparently I was not the only one who was thinking along those lines, because there was definitely a note of skepticism in the inspector's voice as he said, "And I assume if we attempt to find this good woman and her husband, there will be no problem doing so?"

She looked faintly hurt. "I can't imagine there would be. I intend to return myself later today with some gifts to thank them for their kindness. You're welcome to come along."

The inspector did not look up from jotting down his notes. "And this household did not possess a telephone?"

"I don't know." She sounded a little defiant now. "I didn't ask. All I know is that I was desperate to get back here. I knew Alex would be frantic. As soon as I was able to stand, I asked the gentleman to drive me home. He had a jeep. He took me to the house, and the housekeeper told me what was happening here. Of course I came as soon as I changed."

And shampooed and blow-dried that gorgeous hair, and applied make up to be ready for the cameras, and polished her nails. I knew I was thinking what everyone else in the room was thinking: if her story could be sold by the truckload, it would fertilize every lawn on the island.

I said, apropos of absolutely nothing, "Cocoa must have been glad to see you."

Okay, so I knew perfectly well it was not my place to say anything, particularly anything as ridiculously out-of-the-blue as that. But it was worth the scowl from the lawyer and the raised eyebrows from Miles to see her go, for a brief instant, off-script.

She stared at me. It was not a friendly look. "What?"

"Your dog," I said helpfully. "Cocoa. He's been insane without you. He must have been so happy to see you when you got back."

She scrambled to recover from her confusion. "Well, of course. Of course he was. But no happier than I was to see him. Of course, the main thing on my mind was Alex, and all the confusion my disappearance must have caused. That was the main thing I was worried about."

I said, "Well, I'm glad he made it home all right."

She just stared at me.

I maintained my sweet smile. "Because he ran away last night and as of this morning he was still missing."

Rachelle's stare turned cold. "Excuse me," she said. "Who are you?"

Susan spoke up. "He came home," she said. "A few hours ago. Cocoa came home."

Okay, so now I felt a little foolish. I said, "Oh. Well, that's good. Great human interest story. Your dog comes home in time to greet your return from the dead. I'm Raine Stockton, by the way," I added, answering her question. "I'm a huge fan of your work." Among all the other lies that had been told in the past few minutes, this one seemed right at home.

The inspector turned his gaze from me back to Rachelle. "One more question, Madame, if I may."

She composed herself and looked at him pleasantly.

"What is the name of this new film of yours?"

She started to answer, seemed to reconsider, and wet her lips with the tip of her tongue. She glanced at her husband, who remained impassive. Staring at her.

She looked back at the inspector, set her shoulders, and replied calmly, "*Missing.* The title of my new film is *Missing.*"

After that, really, there was nothing more to say.

Miles was tense and silent as we waited under the bougainvillea-laden portico for the rental car to be brought around. I ventured a glance at him. "I guess I should have stayed out of it."

"Yes," he agreed shortly. "We both should have."

And then he glanced at me with a breath of apology. "Sorry, babe." His hand caressed my back briefly, and dropped. "I'm not mad at you. I'm just pissed off in general. I don't like being played. Again."

I was a little confused by that. "Do you think that's what Alex was doing? Playing you? Why?"

Instead of answering, he asked, "What was that about the dog, anyway?"

I said irritably, "That woman spent the past two days in a hotel room somewhere on the other side of the island, and if you want my opinion, Cocoa was probably with her. I thought I could trip her up if she didn't know Cocoa had run away, and I almost did too. I mean, look at her. Look at *me*." I gestured head to toe, and Miles did.

"Looking." He smiled. "Feeling less pissed."

I ignored that for the sake of making my point. But I did like the way he smiled. "My skin is burned to a crisp, my hair is like a Brillo pad, even my eyes are a different color—and that's just from a few hours playing in the surf while wearing sunscreen. There's no way she lay passed out on the beach until some peasant family found her, much less lay unconscious from dehydration for two days. Could she even have swum to shore from the reef? How far is it? Who makes up stuff like that?"

Miles lifted one shoulder. "Maybe. If she's supposed to be an Olympic-class swimmer, maybe she could do it. Anyway, it doesn't matter whether it's true. She could have said she spent the last two days in the belly of a whale and as long as the police can't prove she didn't, she's off the hook."

"All for a publicity stunt for a movie!" I shook my head in disgust. "Who *does* that?"

"Welcome to the glamorous world of the rich and stupid."

The valet pulled up in the red Peugeot and bounced around the car to open the door for me.

Miles pressed a bill into his hand and got behind the wheel.

"Do you really think Alex was in on this?" I asked as he pulled onto the narrow, crowded road that led back to the villa.

"He had to be, the cocky son of a—" A little yellow Smart Car darted in front of us and Miles blasted the horn. The other driver flung his hand out of the window with a universal sign that did not mean *I'm sorry*. Miles barely seemed to notice, scowling behind his sunglasses over matters of much more import. "That's why he wasn't worried about being arrested. He probably planted the damaged regulator himself, just to add drama to the story. I'm guessing they had the whole big reveal lined up for that wake Amanda was planning for Wednesday, but when the police took Alex in yesterday, they had to move the timetable up. If they had pulled this in the US, they'd have a line out the door trying to sue them by now. Probably why they didn't try it there."

I said, "Funny that Alex would go to all this trouble to help promote her movie when she was getting ready to divorce him."

"Maybe this was her condition for staying with him."

"Maybe. It's just that—well, if Rachelle Denison is already Hollywood royalty, what does she need a stunt like this for? Isn't promoting a movie usually something a producer does?"

He was thoughtful for a moment. "Yeah." Then he reached across the console and squeezed my knee. "Do you want to make me very happy? Talk about something else."

I said, "Okay." But I was pretty sure he wouldn't like my choice of topics. "What happened between you and Susan? Why did you divorce?"

I think it was at that moment I knew why I would never feel comfortable in a place like this, for all its glamour and pristine beaches and water so clear you could see the bottom. Sunglasses. The sun was so bright there was no room for shadows, but sunglasses concealed more than shadows ever could. I would have given all I owned at that moment just to see his eyes.

He took his hand off my knee, presumably to make a turn, and he was silent for just long enough to make me think he might not answer. "Irreconcilable differences," he said.

"After eight months?"

I felt, rather than saw the shutter close over his face. "I didn't cheat on her, if that's what you're asking. I am now, and always have been, the perfect serial monogamist."

I supposed that was what I was asking. Asked and answered, but I couldn't let it go. "Did she cheat on you?"

"Not that I know of."

"Then what—"

"Oh, for God's sake, Raine, what difference does it make? It was a long time ago. We were different people back then. I've had another marriage and a kid since then. I can't even remember."

That, I knew in the marrow of my bones, was a lie.

I turned my face to look out the side window. The traffic crept along the winding little hillside road. I kept remembering the way Susan's face had softened when she first had seen him this morning. The way he had looked at her, and not Alex, during the press conference.

After a long time, he spoke again. "My first wife's name was Cynthia," he said. "It was an impulse military marriage, and lasted three years because I spent two of them in a war zone. Melanie's mother was Therese. We got married because she was pregnant. It was all about passion with us, about pushing the boundaries, and it ended because she eventually pushed the boundaries too far and slept with another guy. It lasted five years, which was probably five years too long, but it gave me Mel and it was worth it. Susan was…" He hesitated, but still did not look at me. "Susan was a mistake. We should never have gotten married. We were friends, and probably should have kept it that way." There was more, but he didn't say it. What he didn't say rang between us.

And, to be perfectly honest, I didn't want to hear it. Perhaps because I was afraid that the unspoken truth would break my heart.

So I just smiled a little and said, "I could really use a nap before dinner. This has been the most exhausting vacation I've ever been on."

He seemed to relax marginally. "And it's only Day Two." He glanced at me. "Are we okay?"

Another quick smile. "Yeah, sure. Everything's fine."

I was getting good at convincing people of that. Maybe one day soon I'd even be able to convince myself.

❦ ❦ ❦ ❦ ❦ ❦

CHAPTER EIGHT

While Miles put the car away, I followed the sound of voices through the house and out to the pool deck to discover my dog making an absolute fool of himself over the fellow who had introduced himself as Rick, Cocoa's dog walker. Rita and Melanie were chatting with him while Cisco, flat on his back and splay-legged, enjoyed the ecstasy of a chest rub. I stopped, surprised, and said, "Hi. This is weird. I just had drinks with your boss." And more, a lot more, which, if they had had the television on they would no doubt already know. Clearly they had not.

Rick stood up, and Cisco rolled over, got to his feet, and trotted over to me, tail wagging affably. I dropped to my knees and hugged him, burying my face in the sweet sunny golden smell of him, loving the wriggling enthusiasm with which he greeted me, the shape of his muscles, the silk of his fur, even the smell of his hot-dog scented breath. Grounding myself in him for even those few seconds took away all the ugliness, shock and stress of the previous two hours, gathering up the negativity like a magnet gathers metal shavings. That's what dogs do, that's why we love them. They make bad things go away. I couldn't help thinking about Rachelle, coming home after a two-day absence—even if it hadn't been the near-death experience she had professed—to the dog she loved. Would her reunion with Cocoa after two days have been any less enthusiastic than mine was with Cisco after an absence of only two hours? Yet she had barely seemed to remember it.

"Hey, Raine," Melanie said excitedly, bounding to her feet. "Rick came looking for Cocoa. I told him Cisco was a search and rescue dog and that he could probably find him in no time flat, but Grandma said I should ask you first. So what do you say? Can we take Cisco out searching? Did you bring his gear?"

I stood up, looking at Rick, thoroughly confused now. "Oh," I said. "I thought he had come home. That's what Susan said."

He looked startled, then recovered quickly. "Really? That's great news. I hadn't heard." He laughed a little uneasily. "I guess we can call off the search."

Melanie looked disappointed. "Too bad. Cisco could've found him in a flash."

I told Melanie, "Probably just as well. Cisco's on vacation, and I'm really not sure he's licensed to work in the French West Indies."

She saw the quirk of my smile, and grinned back, patting Cisco's shoulder. "Maybe next time, dude," she told him, and she cheered. "Say, that means Cocoa and Cisco can have their play date after all! We're going to the beach after dinner. Why don't you bring Cocoa down?"

Rick said, "I don't know. I'd have to check with Mr. Barry."

I was dying to tell my news, but Melanie went on happily, "Raine, wait until you see the new trick I taught Cisco. We've been working on it all afternoon. Watch this."

She took a step back, held up her palm, and said, "Cisco, high five!"

Cisco, standing between Melanie and me, almost knocked me over in his enthusiastic leap onto his back legs. He swiped at Melanie's hand with his paw, missed, and bounced down on all fours. She tried again. "High five!" and this time she stepped closer, so that when Cisco jumped up his paw automatically hit Melanie's hand. She was really getting good at this, and I applauded them both, laughing, while Melanie rewarded Cisco with a hot dog treat.

"Good job!" I exclaimed. "Both of you."

"Want to see it again?"

"I do," I assured her. "But first, I wanted to tell you all something."

I took a breath, looking from Rita to Rick, enjoying my moment of importance. "Cocoa's not the only one who came home," I said. "You won't believe who just showed up at Alex Barry's press conference. His wife. Turns out Rachelle Denison wasn't dead after all."

Rita whipped off her sunglasses and sat up straight. "What?"

Melanie said, "You mean the drowned lady didn't drown? Hey, maybe she was a werewolf after all! Cool."

Rita said, "Are you serious? After two days? How is that possible?"

But Rick just stood there, looking astonished. When he noticed my gaze on him he managed, "I— is that right? That's wonderful news. For Cocoa. And Mr. Barry. He must be so relieved."

Rita demanded impatiently, "Raine, really! Don't keep us in suspense! What happened?"

I turned my gaze from Rick back to Rita. "She says she washed up on a beach somewhere and has spent the past two days being nursed back to health by a French couple, but the prevailing theory is that it was all a publicity stunt for her new movie."

"Oh, for heaven's sake!" Rita sank back onto her lounge chair and replaced her sunglasses with a look of contemptuous disbelief on her face that mirrored my own. "These people will stop at nothing."

There was a plate of nibbles and a frosty pitcher of what looked to be pink lemonade on the table under the shade. I helped myself to a date stuffed with gorgonzola. Fabulous. I noticed a cellophane-wrapped package tied with paw print ribbon next to the snack platter and picked it up.

"Actually, that's the main reason I stopped by." Rick stepped forward, making what appeared to be a valiant effort to recover his equilibrium. "Things were a little, well, hectic when I was setting up and I forgot to leave that. Deer antlers," he explained as I examined the contents through the cellophane. "Dogs love them, but be careful not to let him chew them all at one time. Also, there's a card listing our services. Dog walking, pet sitting, day care, even grooming and massage sessions, all part of the service. Any time you're going to be gone for the day, just give me a call and I'll be happy to come by and let him out, or take him on a run, whatever you like."

Melanie put a possessive hand on Cisco's head. "We never leave Cisco. He goes everywhere we do."

As though I would really trust Cisco to a dog-walker who had already lost one golden retriever. I smiled anyway, and said, "Thanks, but she's right. I might take you up on the grooming services, though. And I really loved the way you set up Cisco's room. That was a nice touch."

He smiled briefly, and suddenly seemed in a hurry to get going. "Well, it was nice to see you all. You too, Cisco." He gave Cisco a perfunctory scratch behind the ears and Cisco grinned up at him. "Just call the number on the card if there's anything we can do for you. Bye now."

He hurried down the path to the front drive, and Rita waited until he was out of earshot to observe, "California. He's definitely from California."

I poured myself a glass of lemonade and regaled Rita with the details of our afternoon while Melanie scrolled through a list of entries about Rachelle Denison on her electronic tablet, occasionally speaking up to apprise us of some particularly salient piece of information, like how many stars her last two movies had gotten—more than the first two—and how much money she had purportedly been paid for signing for the new one, which was less than I imagined, although still more than a dog trainer could expect to make in multiple lifetimes.

"She's twenty-nine years old," Melanie reported, "but not for long. Her birthday is tomorrow. Hey, here it is, on Entertainment News."

Melanie turned the tablet around so that we could see the video of the press conference I'd just attended. It was clearly unedited footage and the report was brief; I was sure they would have a much more polished version by air time on the national news.

"She certainly does look cool and collected," observed Rita. "But her husband doesn't look particularly pleased, does he?"

"I think he's supposed to be looking stunned."

"He's doing a pretty good job of it, for someone who isn't a professional."

"The only thing I wish is that she had hung around long enough for some reporter to ask how she had time to get her nails done."

Rita chuckled at that and sat back, reaching for a canapé. "What I don't understand," she added in a moment, frowning thoughtfully, "is why someone would report seeing a body being tossed overboard, if there was no body to dispose of."

"People get a little hysterical when something like this happens," I said with a shrug. "They see things that were never really there at all, or the things they thought were perfectly innocent at the time suddenly look ominous. Maybe it was a fisherman throwing back a catch, or tossing out garbage illegally."

"Or something else illegal," volunteered Melanie helpfully, "like a bale of marijuana or maybe even a cargo box filled with cocaine."

Melanie's current ambition was to join the DEA and train drug-detection dogs. It was an ambition I knew Miles did not like to encourage, but apparently her grandmother had not received the same memo.

"That's an awful lot of cocaine," Rita said. "What kind of self-respecting drug dealer would toss that much money overboard?"

"Oh, he wouldn't be tossing it," Melanie countered, warming to her theory. "He would be stashing it for his partner to come pick it up in one of those fast little cigarette boats and run it to Miami. We're right on the drug route, you know."

"I didn't know that," I said, intrigued.

"Oh, sure. Bogotá, the Philippines, Miami. Isn't that right, Dad?"

Of course Miles had chosen that moment to join us. He had changed to his beach clothes, and I could tell by the expression on his face that the last thing he wanted to talk about was the drug trade.

"Geography," I tried to cover quickly. "We were just talking about the geography of the western Caribbean."

Cisco, who had planted himself hopefully between Melanie and me, watching for dropped snacks, bounced over to greet Miles. Miles bent to pet him, giving me a skeptical, "Hmm-mmm."

"And also about Rachelle Denison," supplied Melanie helpfully. "We think she's a total phony."

"I wouldn't disagree with you there, sweetheart." He straightened up, took a shrimp from the chilled bowl on the table, and fed it to Cisco. Cisco gobbled it down and looked at him worshipfully.

"Hey!" I objected.

He tilted a raised eyebrow at me. "Vacation," he reminded me.

"Hey Dad, want to see Cisco's new trick?"

"Can't think of anything I'd rather do."

Melanie scrambled to her feet, took her stance, and this time when she commanded, "High five!" Cisco struck her palm with perfect precision. We all laughed and applauded, and Miles gave him another shrimp. What dog wouldn't like that game? Melanie tried it three more times, with three more shrimp, until I complained, only half joking, "Save some for me, will you?"

Miles grinned, wiped his hands on a paper napkin, and said, "Okay guys, let's take a break. Speaking of shrimp, where would you ladies like to go for dinner?"

"Oh dear," his mother said. "I thought you and Raine had plans, so I called the concierge service to bring dinner for Melanie and me."

"Spaghetti from Embargo," Melanie added, "the best in the *world*." She looked at her grandmother hopefully. "You could order more."

Miles glanced at me ruefully. "Actually, I did have a plan, and it sounded great this morning. I thought you might enjoy a sunset dinner on the reef, but given that we've just spent the entire afternoon listening to stories about deadly diving accidents on the reef..." He shrugged. "Maybe not such a fun way to spend the evening after all."

But I was interested. "Do you mean the same reef where Alex and Rachelle went diving?"

His tone was guarded. "That's the one."

"Are you planning to push me overboard?"

"That depends. Are you planning to talk about Rachelle Denison all night?"

I grinned. "I'm a strong swimmer. And you've got a dinner date."

Melanie and Miles went down to the beach for another paddle board lesson, but I was content to settle in the shade with Cisco and Rita, the platter of goodies within reach and a glass of white wine in hand. I am really more of a beer girl, but when in Rome, I suppose. I gave Cisco one of the deer antlers, and he crunched it up in no time flat, looked at me hopefully for another, then settled under my chair with a huge disappointed sigh when he saw nothing more was forthcoming. I could feel his watchful eyes, though, waiting for a dropped cracker or another tasty shrimp.

Rita said, "I hope you don't feel you have to sit here with me, Raine. If you'd rather go to the beach…"

"Miles and Melanie need some father-daughter time," I said, stretching out in the lounge chair and kicking off my sandals. "And I could use the rest." And then I glanced at her quickly. "But don't let me keep you here. If you'd rather be doing something else…"

She laughed, acknowledging the mild awkwardness of two people who didn't know each other very well trying to be nice. I grinned back, and the silence that fell between us was easier this time. She sipped her wine and I stretched my toes out to the sun and enjoyed the ocean breeze. In a moment, I said, "Do you mind if I ask you about Susan?"

"Not at all." She seemed unsurprised and unconcerned. "But I'm afraid I can't tell you very much. To be perfectly honest, I only met her once before the wedding." She frowned a little, thoughtfully. "She was an odd type. Nice enough, but I don't know, reserved. Very ambitious. Of course, Miles is ambitious too, which should have made them well suited, I guess, but sometimes it doesn't work that way. I can't really explain it, but I always had a peculiar feeling about her. It just seemed like a strange match to me, and I remember thinking at the time…" She glanced at me with an expression of rueful apology in her eyes. "It's awful of me, I know, but I remember thinking at the wedding that I'd be surprised if the marriage lasted until Christmas. And I was right. It didn't."

"Was it a bitter divorce?"

"Not at all, at least as far as I knew. Miles never talked about it much. He seemed… I don't know. Embarrassed about the whole thing. He doesn't usually make impulsive decisions, and I suppose he doesn't like to be reminded about the impulsive marriage that didn't work out."

"Do you think…" I ventured a careful look at her, worried I was about to go too far, "do you think he might still have feelings for her?"

She gave a startled laugh. "Oh my, I shouldn't think so. In fact, I'm sure of it. As for how she might feel about him, on the other hand…" She shrugged. "It was odd, don't you think, that she should come to Miles to help her brother out of trouble?"

I gave a decisive nod of agreement. "I do think so. But even odder that Miles was actually willing to do it."

"Oh, I don't know about that." She sipped her wine, unconcerned. "That actually makes a bit more sense to me."

"That he would loan money to an ex-wife and a man he doesn't trust?"

She chuckled. "That he would want to keep his options open. I would have been very surprised if he hadn't at least followed up. He's naturally curious." She smiled at me. "Like you."

I blushed a little. "I guess I really shouldn't be grilling you about your son behind his back."

She waved a dismissive hand. An emerald glittered on her finger and I knew without asking that it had been a gift from Miles. "He left us alone together. What else should he expect?"

I laughed, and knew she was right. Miles rarely did anything without being fully aware of the consequences.

She dipped a shrimp in cocktail sauce, guarding her white shirt with a paper napkin. "Miles tells me you were married to a policeman."

So now it was my turn. I nodded. "And my uncle was the sheriff for thirty years before that. I guess that's why I tend to ask too many questions."

"There's no such thing as too many questions," she replied, "as long as you're asking the right ones."

I ventured a small, puzzled smile. "Funny. That sounds like something my father used to say. He was a judge."

"Yes." Her eyes twinkled, and she reminded me very much of her son at that moment. "Miles mentioned you come from an impressive family of defenders of the law."

I tried to smile but it felt uncomfortable and sad. "I used to think so." I looked for a moment at my barely touched glass of wine. Then, without knowing I was going to say anything at all, I added, "When my father died he was the most respected man in the county, maybe even in the state. The governor came to his funeral. He had the kind of reputation on the bench that made you think the words 'honest' and 'fair' had been invented to describe his courtroom. But it turns out he let an innocent man go to prison to cover up his own adultery, and in the process he broke so many laws and betrayed so many people I can't even count them all. It kind of makes you wonder what you can believe in after that, you know?"

I glanced at Rita, but she said nothing. She didn't pretend to understand, or make meaningless sympathetic noises. She just waited for the rest of the story. I figured I might as well tell it.

"The worst part was," I said, "that the woman he was having an affair with all those years—the one he was covering up—was my mother's best friend. No," I corrected myself in a sharp, tight voice, "the worst part was that she was my best friend. She was at our table every Sunday and every holiday since I was a little girl. She gave me my first golden retriever. She stood up for me at my wedding. After Mother died, she was the one I went to with all my problems, and all the good things too. It was her idea to start the kennel business, not mine, and she taught me everything I know about dogs. We worked together, we trained together, we traveled together. I told her everything. And all the time she was keeping this secret from me. This huge, ugly secret." I took a sip of the wine, but it tasted sour in my mouth. I put the glass on the table. "You know what's funny is that I can't imagine what my life would have been like without her. I mean, every part of it is connected to her in one way or another, and now when I look back, it feels like my whole life was just a lie."

Rita said, "How did you find out?"

I shrugged uncomfortably. "She told me, a few weeks back. She never would have said anything at all if it hadn't been about to come out in a police investigation. I don't know. Maybe I would have been better off if she hadn't."

"That must have been a horrible conversation to have. What do you say to a confession like that?"

I picked up my glass, and put it down again. "I think I said, 'Get out of my house'. She did, and that was it. Everything else was just paperwork." Again I shrugged. "She called a couple of times before she moved to Florida, but I just deleted the messages without listening to them."

Rita sipped her wine quietly, gazing out over the pool and the ocean beyond. Cisco snored softly under my chair. She said after a moment, "You know Miles's father was an alcoholic. It's dreadful, living with that disease. For years after he died I wouldn't allow alcohol in the house, or even go to parties where it was served. And then one day it struck me. The man with the drinking problem was dead and gone, but he was still controlling me. His mistakes were defining my life, not my own." She smiled. "It turns out I enjoy a glass of wine now and then, and I like going to Christmas parties where eggnog is served. It's a small thing, I know, but it's a shame to miss out on even one small thing because of someone else's problem. Something that didn't even have anything to do with you."

She looked at me. "What your father did was despicable, Raine. And as for your friend—in some ways that was even worse. I don't know if you can forgive them for it. But it's worth trying, because you're not doing it for them. You're doing it for you."

I said, "Has Miles ever forgiven his father?"

She lifted her glass again. "I don't think so. Instead, he buys me diamonds and beach houses, and although there's definitely something to be said for that..." The flash of her smile had an undertone of regret to it, like the sour taste that lay beneath the brightness of my wine. "What he's really doing is trying to rewrite the past. And that's pointless, isn't it? All you can do is to treasure the good things, and learn to live with the rest."

Cisco stirred beneath my chair, stretching forth his front legs and yawning broadly before crawling out. He shook himself, spraying tiny motes of gold-dusted hair into the air, and turned to me with a happy, tail-waving grin that spoke of nothing but his joy at seeing me again. I couldn't help grinning back as I dropped my hand to his head, massaging his ear. He was definitely one of the good things.

I helped myself to a shrimp from the platter, then served one to my dog. He gulped it down ecstatically and then sniffed the deck for dropped crumbs. "So," I said, picking up my wine again, "what do you suppose one wears to have a sunset dinner on a sailboat in the Caribbean?"

CHAPTER NINE

Don't get me wrong. I'm as romantic as the next girl, and Miles, if I haven't mentioned it already, is one sexy guy, particularly the way he looked that night in jeans and a silver silk shirt that was the exact color of his eyes. But by the time we parked at the marina that evening, I wasn't thinking as much about lobster and champagne under the stars as I was about tides and currents and how far the reef really was from shore, and what might have inspired Rachelle Denison to make up such an outrageous story. That is just the way my mind works. I would be going home in a few days to my dogs and my kennel and my mostly ordinary life, but this incident was likely to be referenced more than once between now and the time Rachelle's new movie came out. It would be fun to be able to say I had actually been to the place where the whole thing started.

The sun sets late in the Caribbean, and by the time we left the house, Melanie, Rita, and Cisco had already had their dinner and were preparing for one last walk on the beach before settling down to watch a movie on television. The azure sky was overlaid with a faint trace of pink clouds as we walked down the dock, and the breeze was warm and salty, ruffling through my hair pleasantly. Miles looked tanned and relaxed and he smelled of Polo, which had recently become my favorite scent. He held my hand. A few of the dogs who had greeted Cisco so enthusiastically during the day peered over their rails to watch us pass, but we didn't stir up nearly as much excitement without Cisco along. In the distance, some poor dog whose owners had locked him in the cabin while they went to dinner barked the bark of the lonely and the bored.

I said, "I should call Melanie and remind her to keep Cisco on leash if they're going to the beach."

"You reminded her twice. You also reminded Mom. She'll think you don't trust her."

"I trust Melanie fine. It's Cisco I'm a little iffy on."

Miles put his arm around my waist and drew me close, hip to hip. "Do you know why I brought you here?"

"For a vacation?"

"Right. And what do you suppose people go on vacation to do?"

I pretended to think about that. "Relax?"

"Wrong., People go on vacation to be, for a few days, somebody they don't get to be the rest of the year."

"And what do you want me to be?" I teased him, bumping his shoulder playfully with mine. "Tall, blond and leggy?"

He threaded his fingers briefly through my tangle of curls which were, in fact, beginning to take on a blond tinge, then let his fingers rest upon my neck, caressing. "I prefer mid-sized brunettes, and I like your legs the way they are. This is what I want you to be."

He surprised me by taking out his phone and turning it toward me. A picture of me, holding up a blue ribbon with Cisco by my side, filled the screen. I had never looked worse—tangled hair held back by a baseball cap, no makeup, sweaty, bloody and bruised, grinning like a banshee. Instinctively I put my hand out to cover the screen. "Miles! I can't believe you kept that picture."

"It's my screen-saver," he said.

I stared at him. "I hate you."

He winked and kissed my hair, then put the phone away. "I want you to be the girl you were when you won that ribbon. You had a black eye and a bloody nose, but you were laughing. I haven't seen you laugh like that since that day."

My step faltered a bit as I looked up at him. I wanted to deny it, but I thought he might be right. And what kind of man would take a woman—and her dog— on a Caribbean vacation just because he wanted to see her laugh? My voice was a little subdued when I said, after a moment, "I know why you really invited your mother here."

"Oh?" His tone was cautious.

"So that I would have someone to talk to."

His smile was gentle as he caressed the back of my neck. "Family is important," he said. "Everybody needs one."

My throat got suddenly, ridiculously tight, and my voice was husky as I looked up at him. I probably should have said something profound, but all I could manage was, "You know something? You're a really good boyfriend."

"A fact I sometimes think you don't fully appreciate," he agreed.

I slipped my arm around his waist and pressed my head against his shoulder, and the moment might have turned really sloppy except that I happened to glance up just then and I noticed the deck of the boat we were passing. My step slowed. A man was sitting there at a small table with a bottle of scotch and a glass in front of him, staring, not at the ocean or the gorgeous sunset that was beginning to glow overhead, but at the dock where we were. "Miles... isn't that Alex Barry?"

The reason I was unsure was because he seemed to have aged ten years in the few hours since we had seen him. The glow of the sun etched unflattering lines on his face and his eyes looked blank, glazed over. Except for rhythmically lifting the glass to drink, he was motionless.

Miles glanced in the direction of my gaze. "Quite possibly. That's his boat."

I started to wave and call out, but Miles caught my hand. "Whoa, baby, this isn't downtown Mayberry. Leave the man alone."

I pulled my hand away, a little annoyed about the Mayberry remark, although I shouldn't have been. I was a small town girl with small town values and small town curiosity; that was supposed to be one of the things Miles liked about me. "I think he's drunk," I said.

"I think so too, which is why we're going to leave him alone."

He urged me forward, and I took a few steps before looking back. "He doesn't even see us," I observed.

"Good."

"I wonder why he's not at home, celebrating with Rachelle."

"I've never known why Alex does anything."

I watched as Alex Barry refilled his glass. To the brim. Of course this shouldn't have concerned me, particularly after the stunt Alex and Rachelle had pulled that afternoon. But one of the most inconvenient things about having small town values is that in a small town, we don't leave the wounded behind—even when they're on the other team.

"Miles," I said, a little worried, "I don't think anyone else is on the boat. He's been drinking all day. You should go see if he's okay."

A flash of impatience crossed his face. "I don't even like the man. And I particularly don't like him right now."

"What if he tries to drive home?" I insisted. "Or take the boat out?"

His lips tightened, but I could see a wavering in his eyes. I managed to put just the right mix of plea, charm and promise into my own expression. I had been around Cisco long enough to get it right. "It will only take a minute," I persuaded, caressing his arm.

He muttered an oath under his breath and turned back to the boat. "Good evening, Alex," he called. "Everything okay?" His tone, to the passing observer, might even have been construed as pleasant.

Alex did not answer for the longest moment. He just stared at us. Then he lifted his arm in a sloppy beckoning motion and called back, "Come aboard."

Miles gave me an annoyed look. "Great," he said. "My dinner is waiting four slips down."

I responded with a shrug and an apologetic smile, and followed him across the ramp onto Alex Barry's boat.

Alex lifted his glass to us as we approached. "You brought your pretty lady. Welcome, pretty lady." Alex's voice was clear, his enunciation precise, and his gaze stone hard, expressionless. "Can I get you a drink?"

Before I could answer, Miles said, "I doubt you could stand up long enough to get anything."

Alex laughed. "I believe you may be right. Why don't you sit down, then?"

Miles glanced around. "Is anyone here with you?"

A tight little smile. "Besides yourself?"

Miles took out his phone. "I'm calling a car for you. You shouldn't be on the water."

Alex sipped his drink with movements that were as controlled and precise as his voice. "Where, pray tell, should I be?"

173

Miles started to dial. "How about at home with your wife?"

"That woman," said Alex, lifting his glass again, "is not my wife."

Miles didn't bother to respond, but Alex seemed just serious enough to arouse my curiosity. "What?"

"You heard correctly, my dear," replied Alex. He took another sip of his drink. "The woman you saw this afternoon is not the woman I married. She is not Rachelle Denison."

I sat down at the table across from Alex, intrigued. "Why do you say that?"

"Because it's true." Another sip. "The woman is an imposter."

I glanced at Miles, but he didn't even look up from his phone. I said, "Why would someone pretend to be your wife when she's not?"

He lifted his glass to me again in a slight toast. "That, my lovely, is the question of the hour."

I tried again. "What makes you think she's not your wife?"

One of the lines beside his mouth deepened, that was the only indication of what was supposed to be a smile. "Because she told me so."

Even Miles glanced up from his text at that.

I looked at him closely, but how could I read anything on a face like that? His eyes were so glassy that I could actually see the colors of the clouds reflected in them. "She told you that she was not Rachelle Denison," I said, just to be clear.

He waved a hand in a slight dismissive gesture. Unfortunately it was the hand that held his glass, and some of the scotch splattered on the table. "I accused her," he said. He swallowed more scotch. "She just laughed and said, 'prove it'. That's what she said. *Prove it*." He drank again. "But without the real Rachelle, I can hardly do that, can I?" He shrugged. "Then Susan came back in the room and she was back in the role again, hanging on me, playing out her story, talking about the press conference she was going to give in the morning, calling her agent... I couldn't stay.   Couldn't watch it." Another drink. "So here I am."

I glanced at Miles. He was checking the screen on his phone. I said, "What do you think happened to the real Rachelle?"

"I know damn well what happened to her." His tone was harsh. "I told you. I told everyone. She drowned. But without a body I can't prove that. Do you know why burials at sea are so efficient, Miss Pretty Lady?" He drank again. "Marine life and salt water can strip a carcass bare in a matter of hours. That's the truth."

I said, "Have you told the police about your suspicions?"

"Of course he hasn't told the police." Miles put his phone away, his expression impatient. "The next time he sets foot in a police station it will be because he's under arrest for fraud. Alex, you're drunk and I've had enough of your drama for one day. A car is on its way for you, and if you take my advice, you'll get in it and go home, where you will at least pretend to be glad to see the wife you supposedly thought was dead for the past two days. Because after the stunt you pulled, she may be the only friend you've got left."

A vague and rather tragic smile touched Alex Barry's lips. He drank again. "He's right, you know," he told me. "I can't go to the police. She made sure of that. It really is the perfect crime."

Miles said, "Raine, let's go. I want to get the boat out of the slip while we still have daylight."

I stood reluctantly, mostly because I suspected he was about to pull me to my feet and drag me off the boat, and that would have been a mistake neither one of us wanted him to make. I followed him to the ramp.

"He didn't come back," Alex said.

I looked back at him. "What?"

"The dog," he said, gazing out at nothing at all. "He didn't come back."

I started to say something, but felt the pressure of Miles's hand on my back and held my tongue until we were off the boat. "Miles," I said, "that doesn't make sense."

"Of course it doesn't." It seemed to me he was walking faster, and the weight of his hand against my shoulder blade forced me to keep up.

"I mean, Rachelle Denison is a well-known person. People would know if it wasn't her."

"Of course they would."

"Susan thought it was her. Everyone at the press conference thought it was her."

"That's because it was her."

"But why would he say—"

"Raine, I don't know." He voice was tense and hard. "What I do know is that he's got some other scheme going on and he's trying to pull you into it and that's not going to happen. Now, I did the Christian thing, I called a car for him, and unless he falls off the boat in the next five minutes, he's going to be someone else's problem, at least for tonight. So can we just go?"

I said, "Wow. You really don't like him."

"Let's just say this is not the way I pictured spending my vacation."

"Still," I murmured thoughtfully, "it really would be the perfect crime."

Miles stopped, turned to me, and took both my shoulders. He said, very distinctly, "There has been no crime. And even if there had been, it has nothing to do with you, or me, or this glorious sunset we are missing because of some deranged megalomaniac and his drunken fantasies. Agreed?"

"But—"

He kissed me. I am not the kind of woman who can be distracted by a kiss, which Miles knows perfectly well, even though he is awfully good at it. But when he said again, "Agreed?" I felt some measure of conciliation on my part was in order. After all, he had gone to some trouble to arrange this evening, and I did appreciate it.

So I smiled and said, "Agreed. The sunset is gorgeous. It's just that... "

He blew out an exasperated breath and let his head fall back briefly in a gesture of surrender. I might have gone on; in fact, I'm sure I would have, but suddenly there was a blast of light, a whooshing sound, and a muffled *boom* that seemed simultaneous with the flash of shock and terror that streaked across Miles's face, and all of that seemed instantaneous with my knees and palms hitting the concrete when Miles pushed me down, sheltering me while embers of the sunset rained down around us in fiery shards.

Dogs barked; people came to the rails of their boats and whipped out their phones; others shouted and ran toward us. Somewhere in the distance there was the whooping sound of an alarm. The acrid smell of black smoke filled the air and blotted the sky. Miles and I knelt together on the pavement, holding on to each other, unable to speak or even move; watching in abject astonishment as his boat went up in flames.

CHAPTER TEN

Three other boats were damaged, fortunately with no one onboard, before the flames were extinguished. Sightseers and boat owners were pushed back to the far end of the dock or into the parking lot, but even from that distance I could tell Miles's boat was unsalvageable. Spotlights and emergency lights gleamed in the puddles on the concrete as darkness fell, and everyone with a cell phone was taking pictures. Fortunately, as someone had observed, the marina was not very crowded this time of year, otherwise the damage could have been much more extensive.

To me the marina seemed plenty crowded as people poured off their expensive yachts and returned from their expensive dinners to gape and point and jostle and shove. That was probably why

I noticed the one figure who was still and quiet while the excitement whirled around him, leaning against a dark limousine with no expression whatsoever on his face and eyes that were cold and dead. It was Alex Barry, and he did not look nearly as drunk as he had appeared when we last met. After a time, he got into the car and the driver took him away. He never once walked the few dozen steps to see if we were okay, or to express his concern to Miles over the boat. He didn't even acknowledge that I was looking at him.

He was, as Miles had indicated more than once, a bastard.

The fire chief—or was it the harbor master?—did not speak English, or he pretended not to, and it took awhile before Miles found someone in authority who did. By this time his frustration was palpable. "I've already told you," he said to the official-looking man in the button-down blue shirt with the clipboard in his hand, "we hadn't even boarded the boat. It had been docked since noon. It was a sail-boat, for God's sake. They don't just explode."

The man nodded importantly. "Indeed, monsieur. But you do store fuel on board?"

Miles looked as though the other man was still speaking French. He said, "Do you mean for the outboard?"

I remembered that Miles had used an outboard engine to maneuver the boat out of the harbor that morning before raising the sails, and again to maneuver it into position before approaching the shallows where we had snorkeled. It made navigating much easier, he'd explained, and was good for an emergency. But how much gasoline could one of those things use?

The important man went on, "*Oui, c'est ca,* but also for cooking, for your food heater, yes?"

Miles frowned. "No. There's no galley onboard, it's a sailboat for the love of—"

"*Mais non.*" He consulted his clipboard. "It would appear that the propane food warmer malfunctioned and ignited the container of gasoline which was kept nearby. You are fortunate, monsieur," he added sternly, "such a malfunction did not occur while you were at sea."

"Food warmer," Miles repeated, and as the angry confusion on his face slowly cleared, I understood as well.

"Dinner was waiting," I said, remembering his complaint when I had insisted we stop to check on Alex. "The concierge service must have used a portable propane stove to keep it warm."

He nodded absently, still frowning. "I've never used them to cater dinner on the boat before."

"Why would they leave an open flame unattended?" I wondered out loud.

His frown only deepened. "A question for the insurance company." He looked at the official. "When can I go onboard and check out the damage for myself?"

"I am afraid that will not be possible, monsieur. The craft is not safe for boarding." The official-looking man handed Miles a paper from his clipboard. "This is an order to have your vessel removed from the marina within five days. Failure to do so will result in significant fines and charges against you. You will also please visit the office of the harbor master at your earliest possible convenience, to review other paperwork." He paused and looked back in the direction of the charred remains of the sailboat. "I am very sorry for your loss, monsieur." His regret sounded genuine. "She must have been a beautiful boat."

Miles agreed heavily, "She was."

The man nodded his head, reminded Miles of the five-day deadline, and departed. I wrapped my hands around Miles's arm and leaned in close in a gesture of comfort, pointing out, "It could have been worse. We could have been onboard."

"We should have been onboard." He looked at me, his expression haunted. "If you hadn't insisted we stop and talk to Alex, we would have been onboard. We might have even been out of the harbor."

"Or," I pointed out, "you might have noticed whatever was wrong with the propane stove and turned it off." I gave a short sharp shake of my head, refusing to go there. "That's the thing about accidents. Second-guessing never makes them any better."

He said, almost to himself, "The reserve fuel was in the storage bench. I can't figure out how..."

He let the sentence trail off but I knew what he was thinking. There were a lot of unanswered questions. And how much gasoline would it have taken to produce an explosion and flash fire like that one, anyway?

Abruptly, almost fiercely, Miles drew me close and kissed my hair. I knew I smelled like smoke and charred gasoline, and so did he. He said, "Let's get you some first aid. And dinner."

The first aid referred to my scraped knee; the cinder-holes in his silk shirt— the one that was the exact shade of his eyes—were much more painful to me. As for dinner... I was really wishing I had stayed home for spaghetti from Embargo.

I mustered a smile. "Maybe a rain check on dinner. Any chance we could call it a night?"

He responded by squeezing my waist, and I leaned into the strong muscles of his chest. "Baby, two great minds with but a single thought."

His phone rang. I knew Miles had blocked all calls for the length of this trip from anyone except his mother, Melanie, or me. I guessed one of them had seen something on the news about the fire at the marina and so, from the expression on his face, did Miles. He answered with a casual, "Hi, Mom. Everything's fine. I was going to call."

But then he was quiet, listening. I saw the tiny muscles in his face go slack, and in the glare of the phosphorescent lights, his lips seemed to lose color. He said hoarsely, "When?"

I stared at him, trying to hear what was being said on the other end of the connection, trying to read his expression. Except for the clatter of voices and the grind of engines and the mutter of equipment all around us, there was silence. It was a silence of the mind, and it seemed to go straight to my heart.

After forever, Miles said, "We're on our way."

He put away his phone and he looked at me. His eyes were two dark orbs that looked through me and saw nothing. He said, "It's Mel." His voice was stunned and laced with disbelief, the voice of a man who never expected to speak the words he was about to say. "She's disappeared."

Your mind goes down all the usual paths. *Misunderstanding. Missed connection. She'll be home before we get there, apologetic and contrite and with a really, really good explanation.* Even though I knew Rita would not have called in a panic if there was a chance any of those things were true. It was dark. It had been dark for almost an hour. And Rita had been searching for Melanie since sunset.

I said things like, "She's a smart girl." *Just a little too independent.* "She knows how to take care of herself." *And she wouldn't just disappear.* "She knows her way around the island." But her phone was lying on her bed where she had left it before she went to the beach that afternoon. She couldn't call for help if she wanted to.

Then there were those other paths, the paths I knew Miles's mind was taking too, the paths I didn't want to explore, couldn't bear to explore. *The daughter of a wealthy man. An island with a foreign government, surrounded by water where anything could—and often did—happen. Do you know why burials at sea are so efficient, Miss Pretty Lady?*

Melanie would never, ever just disappear. Not if she had a choice.

"Okay," I breathed out, hardly aware I was speaking aloud. "Just wait. We don't know the details. It could be simple. Just wait."

The drive to the marina had taken about twenty minutes. The drive home took half that time, and Miles never said a single word.

The lights were blazing all over the house and the grounds when we pulled up. A single police car was out front. It was one of those ridiculous little Euro cars with only one light on top and it wasn't even flashing. I don't know why a detail like that should strike me as so outrageous, but it did.

I don't remember leaving the car. I barreled into the house with my breath dragging in my chest, and Miles a powerful shadow at my side. No scrabbling of claws on the marble floor. No cheerful, "Hi, Raine!" No waving golden tail. Just harsh lights and cold silence and Rita, looking small and vulnerable as she stood in the center of the big room, hugging her arms and talking to the uniformed officer. When she saw Miles, she broke off and rushed to him; he embraced her and they held on to each other, hard, for a long moment before he said, "Tell me."

But because she was his mother, she touched his soot-smudged cheek and noticed the burn holes in his shirt and she said, "What happened?"

"Nothing. A fire at the marina. It doesn't matter. How long has she been gone?"

The officer said, "You are Monsieur Young?"

Miles barely glanced at him. He held his mother's eyes, willing her to stay calm. "What happened?"

Her hand fluttered to her lips and she took half a breath to compose herself. "We took Cisco for a walk on the beach after dinner. We kept him on leash, like you asked, Raine. We didn't go far. It was still light when we got back. Melanie and Cisco ran ahead up the steps, the way they always do. They went through the gate and it closed behind them. I was only a few minutes behind…" She had to stop and I could tell she was trying not to cry. I wanted to tell her it wasn't her fault, that everything was going to be okay, and I wanted to scream at her to go on.

Rita braced herself and continued, "Everything seemed normal at first. The gate was locked, the back doors were open but you know Melanie never closes them. I went inside and called her, but she didn't answer. I—I thought she didn't hear me. We were going to watch a movie, so I made popcorn. Then I realized I didn't hear Cisco."

She glanced at me, but I was okay. I knew I was going to hear this. Melanie wouldn't leave Cisco. Cisco wouldn't leave Melanie. Not if either one of them had a choice.

Rita swallowed hard. "That's when I started looking for them, but I didn't really panic. Not then. I thought Melanie had taken Cisco to the pool, so I checked. I walked all around the grounds, calling them. Then I checked the house, every room. But they were gone."

Okay then. This is what I do. I find missing people. I knew the questions to ask. I knew the steps to take. This is what I do.

I said, "How much time had passed by then since you last saw them?"

She looked uncertain. "I don't know. I might have been five minutes behind them at the beach. It takes four minutes to make popcorn... Maybe fifteen, twenty minutes."

"And then you searched the neighborhood?" Because that's what I would have done.

She nodded. "I thought... I don't know, I thought Cisco might have gotten away from her and she chased him down the street. Or that for some reason she'd decided to take him on a walk outside the gate. I searched and I called until it was too dark to see, and I knocked on doors when I could, and then I came back here but they still weren't home..." Her voice had gotten higher and tighter with every word until finally it broke. She started to cry.

I said, "Was the front door closed?"

She nodded.

"And the front gate?"

"Locked."

Which eliminated the possibility that Cisco had run into the street, or left the property at all of his own volition.

Miles said, "What about the security cameras?"

The policeman spoke up for the first time. "I naturally checked the cameras, monsieur. Unfortunately, they were malfunctioning."

Miles demanded harshly, "What the hell do you mean, malfunctioning?"

"I mean that they do not appear to have recorded anything since late this afternoon. Beyond that, I cannot say. I am not a technician."

In a missing child case, the first twenty-four hours are critical. That's why we have Amber Alerts. I doubted there was an equivalent here on the island, but at least two hours had already passed.

I turned to the officer. "Have you sent out her photograph to every officer on the force?" The beach house was filled with pictures of Melanie. But none of them were with Cisco.

"It is routine mademoiselle, however—"

"You gave him a recent picture, right?" I asked Rita. "And a description of what she was wearing?"

At Rita's affirmative I turned back to the officer. "Make sure it goes out to neighboring islands too, and into every place of business on the island. Meanwhile I need a sectional street map broken down into grids. I need people going door to door, and people on the beach. I need a helicopter with search lights to sweep the beach and the estates we can't get into." *I need my dog.* "Have you even talked to the neighbors? Do you know if there were any strange vehicles around ? Did anyone hear anything?"

The officer was young and smoothed-cheeked, and the indulgent, faintly condescending smile he gave made me want to slap him. "Mademoiselle may have seen too much American television," he said. "Matters such as this, they tend to resolve themselves much more simply than one might imagine."

Miles took an abrupt step toward him and I grabbed his arm, knowing exactly what he was about to do because I wanted to do the same thing. I spoke before Miles could. "Do you know Inspector LeClerk?" I demanded.

He looked startled, and a little less smug than he had before. "*Mais certainment.* But—"

"Call him," I said.

"I hardly think—"

Miles said, very lowly, "Do it. Do everything this young woman tells you to do and do it right now or I will have more than your job, are we very clear on that?"

I waited just long enough to see the young officer, with an angry flush creeping up his cheeks, snatch out his phone and stride toward the door to make the call, then I turned back to Rita. "Where is Cisco's leash?"

She looked at me through wet lashes as though wondering whether I was thinking clearly. "I—I haven't seen it. I don't know."

I made a quick search of the deck and the pool area, the kitchen and both my room and Melanie's. I came back down, breathless, in time to hear the officer say in a stilted tone, "The inspector is on his way, monsieur. However, he asked me to convey to you that we are a small police force with limited resources…"

I had heard those words once too often today, and I interrupted without hesitation. "I think whatever happened occurred before Melanie had time to take Cisco's leash off. She came up the stairs, entered the security code…" I looked at Rita. "The security lock was still working when you came up?"

She nodded and I went on, "She came into the house through the back doors from the deck with Cisco still on his leash, and went out the front door, closing it behind her. Then she left by the front gate, closing it behind her."

The policeman said, with another smug twitch of his lips, "What you are saying, mademoiselle, is that the little girl took her puppy dog for a walk."

Automatically I put my hand out to restrain Miles, but he fortunately did not see the smirk. He had his phone in hand and was dialing a number.

Miles said, "This is a monitored security system. A record is kept of every time the code is entered."

I spoke to the officer very calmly, and quietly enough so that I hoped Miles could not hear from his position across the room, where he had walked to make his call. "Maybe that is what I'm saying. Maybe that's all that happened. But that little girl is ten years old and she's in a foreign country where she doesn't speak the language and it's dark outside." *And all she has to depend on is Cisco*, I added desperately myself, *Cisco, who she thinks is a combination of Lassie and Rin Tin Tin and Super Man but who is in fact just a dog, depending on her to keep him safe... A dog who would get into a car with anyone, anytime, who said "Do you want to go for a ride?", a dog whose heart is so big he can't even imagine that everyone he meets is not as good-intentioned as he is, a dog who only wants to make people happy...*

I tightened every muscle in my body against the sobs that were building up inside me, and I finished in a low, fierce voice, "There is nothing, do you hear me, *nothing* more important than finding that little girl right now. Nothing."

Miles returned to us. The white lines around his mouth were very tight and his eyes were still, but behind those eyes was busyness, thinking, examining, analyzing, postulating, forming and rejecting theories. He was a man who solved problems, who made things happen. And now he was holding himself together by nothing but sheer will.

"The back gate was last opened at 7:43," he said. "The next time the security code was entered was for the front gate, at 9:20."

It took me a moment to understand the implications, as it did Rita. "But—that would be when I let you in." She glanced at the officer, and then back to Miles. "That's not possible. Melanie had been gone for over an hour by then. I entered the code twice for the front gate, once to get out and once to get back in. I looked everywhere. She wasn't on the property. How can that be?"

"It can't be," Miles said grimly. "Sometime between the time Melanie entered the code on the back gate at seven thirty five and the time you entered it at seven forty three someone overrode the security code on the front gate and came onto my property. That person took my daughter."

It was, of course, what we all feared. It was the place your mind goes when you say *Don't go there*. It was the truth none of us wanted to admit into the realm of possibility even though we all knew it was the only truth that made sense.

Inspector LeClerk arrived less than ten minutes later. He seemed unsurprised to see me, and in fact went so far as to assure Miles he had done the right thing in calling. His questions were to the point.

"Do you have any enemies, Mr. Young?"

"Have you traveled to the Middle East in the past twelve months? Brazil? Columbia?"

"How many people knew the security code? Their names, please."

"How much cash US can you raise in twenty four hours?"

That was when Miles, with eyes as hard as flint, said, "As much as it takes."

Rita's hand closed around mine, bone hard, painful.

It was ten twenty-five. Did he have any idea how much time he had wasted already? Twenty four hours, that was all we had. Maybe less. I didn't know how things worked here. It was an island, with multiple escape routes by water, by air, by land. Hiding places I couldn't begin to fathom. Marine life that could strip a carcass bare in a matter of hours.

More than anything in the world at that moment I wanted to be home. I wanted to be home where I knew the rules, with Buck giving orders and Uncle Roe providing back-up and Aunt Mart praying quietly in the background and a dozen sheriff's deputies with flashing blue lights combing the hillside, and the entire tracking club with dogs spread out on the search grid, and every neighbor and church member and friend and relative rallying to help. This place was not where I belonged. I was helpless here. I wanted my dog. *I wanted my dog.*

I had been on a search once, for a woman and her dog who had gone missing on the Appalachian Trail. We found the dog three days later, starving, dehydrated, still trailing his leash. But the body of the missing woman wasn't found for another two weeks. In pieces.

Don't go there, don't go there…

I tried to play out the scene in my mind. Melanie had come into the house. Cisco would have been trailing his leash. If someone was already in the house, he would have known it immediately, he would have led her right to them....

The inspector said, "We are watching the ferry and the air strip. I have called in the gendarmes to search the streets. We will find her, monsieur."

Miles said, "There are over a hundred private boats in the harbor with registries from all over the world. Are you going to search each of them too?" His tone was even, almost reasonable.

I thought about white slavery, about drug trafficking, and about Susan, for some reason, asking Miles for half a million dollars. *How much cash can you raise in twenty four hours?*

"As you know, our resources are limited. I'm afraid that would be impractical."

Cisco would have been trailing his leash. If someone was hiding, that person might have grabbed Melanie before she could scream. It would not have been easy, getting a resistant ten- year- old girl out of the house and into a waiting vehicle with a dog barking and bounding around. What would Cisco have done?

"Then get more resources. Call Interpol." Miles's voice was calm, reasonable. A ticking bomb, about to explode. "Whatever the expense, I'll cover it."

"This is not a case for Interpol at this time. We are doing everything we can, monsieur."

"That's not enough!" The eruption came; eyes flaming, muscles tensing, voice roaring. He surged toward the inspector and when I reached for him he flung me off without even a glance. "It's not enough, you pompous little pissant! This is my daughter, do you understand that? She's been kidnapped! She's been…"

He broke off, almost as though the echo of the words had caught up with him and he was hearing them for the first time, understanding them. Kidnapped. He stood there, nostrils flared, fists clenched, lips compressed, for another long moment. Then he said, very distinctly, "My daughter is not going to be headline news tomorrow morning. She is not going to be the target of an international search. She is not going to be what people think about for the next ten years when they hear the name of this island. It's not going to happen, do you understand me?"

The inspector held his ground, and he held his demeanor. I had to admire him for that. He said somberly, "You may be sure we are agreed on all those points, monsieur. As I was about to say earlier, we are a small security force here on the island but we are very good at what we do. Kindly allow us to do our jobs. You can best assist by remaining calm and being prepared. A call may come."

Or maybe that was not what had happened at all. Maybe they had surprised a burglar. Maybe he had fled through the front door and Cisco had given chase, and Melanie had run after him. Cisco had been trailing his leash.

I said abruptly, "Miles, I need a flashlight. They wouldn't have taken Cisco, they would be trying to get away from him. Cisco is out there somewhere, and with his leash on he couldn't have gotten far. He may be caught on something, but even if he's not, he doesn't know how to find his way back here. He's the only one who knows what really happened, and if someone took her, Cisco has the scent. If I can find him I can find Melanie, or at least get closer than we are now."

Rita got up and left the room. The inspector gave me a skeptical glance. "Mademoiselle, I think it would be better if you did not interfere with the efforts of the gendarmes at this point. We are doing—"

Miles cut him off. " Do you have trained dogs on your team? Are they out there searching right now?"

"I regret to say that our resources do not allow—"

"Then stay out of my way," I said. "I know you're just doing your job but you need to let me do mine." As I spoke I was lacing up the pair of sneakers that I had left on the back deck that afternoon, and tying back my hair. I was still wearing my smudged and torn dinner clothes, but I could not take time to change. Too much time had passed already and I, too, had limited resources in this strange place that wasn't my home. Without my dog, I had no resources at all.

The inspector said to me, not unkindly, "Mademoiselle, I hope I am wrong in this, but you should understand that if in fact the child has been taken, and if those responsible for doing so were clever enough to override your security code and disable the cameras, they also would have disposed of the family dog. I fear your search may be futile."

I stood up, my jaw set. Did he think I hadn't thought of that? *Did he*? I said flatly, "Then they would have shot him at the door."

I pushed past him to meet Rita, who returned silently with two flashlights. She put one in my hand and Miles took the other. She laid a hand gently on his arm, looking up at him with a face that was pinched and drawn and eyes that were filled with pain. For the first time I saw a woman who looked her age. "Miles," she said softly, reluctantly, "shouldn't you call Cynthia? She's Melanie's mother, she should know."

I saw his jaw knot, and I knew, as clearly as if he had spoken it out loud, what he was thinking. Once he made that phone call, it was real. There was no going back from there.

He said briefly, "Not yet." Then, "Mother, you wait here in case she comes back, or someone calls the house. I have my phone. Raine, let's go."

The truth was that I probably could have done better by myself, but one glance at Miles's face and I was not about to object. He needed to be moving, to feel that he was doing something, just as I did. I could only hope that what we were doing was enough.

We went out the front door and into the brilliantly lit lawn toward the front gate. There was only one police car in the drive beside the crookedly parked Peugeot we had left there a lifetime ago. Why weren't there dozens of cars with lights blazing and radios crackling? Had they dusted the keypad for fingerprints? Had they taken the cameras to inspect them for tampering?

I fear your search may be futile.

I said, "We should probably split up. You take the beach, I'll take the streets."

He said lowly, "I should have prepared her for this. I knew it was a possibility. She should have had self-defense lessons, martial arts, I should have made sure she knew how important it was to keep her phone with her. She should have had a panic button. Why didn't I make sure she had a panic button?"

He did not want me to say anything; he just wanted me to listen. But every word he spoke was a tiny dagger in my heart, because he spoke in the past tense.

"I should have been more careful. I should have *known.*"

"Miles." I placed a hand lightly on his arm. He looked startled for an instant, almost as though he had forgotten I was there. "This is not helping. You need to stay focused."

In a moment, he said brusquely, "You're right." He looked at his watch. "Give it forty-five minutes, and meet back here. Is your phone on?"

I nodded. "Check the shadows at the bottom of the beach steps where his leash might be caught. And be sure to stop and wait after you call him to give him time to reach you."

They also would have disposed of the family dog.

The front gate was closed. All the gates were on a sensor system and closed automatically as soon as the person or vehicle cleared the electric eye. Miles punched in the code. The double gates parted slowly.

"Daddy?"

I think at first neither one of us believed the sound. Miles did not move, and for the longest time it seemed my muscles were also frozen; I hardly dared even to breathe as I strained to hear above the rumbling of the gate and the sound of the ocean which suddenly seemed more of a roar than a whisper. And then...footsteps? Breathing? Panting?

"Daddy!"

I swung my flashlight beam toward the sound and Melanie's face appeared out of the shadows, running toward us even as Miles was already running toward her. Her face was red and wet with sweat and tears, her hair disheveled, her tee shirt dirty. But alive. Running toward her father with arms open and sobs stuttering with every step. Miles swept her up, saying something, gasping something, holding her tight, kissing her face, and she wrapped her arms around him, crying, "Daddy, they took him! They took Cisco!"

CHAPTER ELEVEN

The next few moments were filled with noise and clatter and lights and weeping and laughter and movement. That was all I would ever remember about them. The inspector on his telephone, Melanie on the sofa, her own sofa, while Miles wiped her dirty, tear-smudged face with a damp washcloth and Rita pressed a glass of juice into her hand. I dropped down onto one knee and said gently, because someone had to and this was my job, this was what I did, I found people; because I knew what had to be done, I said, "Melanie, are you okay? Did anyone hurt you, or try to hurt you? You're safe now, everything is okay. But you need to tell us if they did."

I saw the darkness come into Miles's eyes and saw Rita go still with dread, but the best moment in my whole life was when Melanie shook her head, wiped her still-running nose with the back of her hand and said, "No. He tied up my hands with tape and put tape over my mouth and eyes and when I cried it was hard to breathe, so I tried not to cry. But he didn't hit me or try to do bad stuff or anything. He just threw me in the back and forgot about me." But then her eyes filled with tears again and she said, "Raine, they took Cisco. I tried to stop them, I did, but they drove away and I couldn't get him back!"

I managed a shaky smile. "It's okay, Mel, the important thing is that you're home safe and you can help find him, okay? Why don't you start by telling us what happened?"

The inspector came over, listening quietly, but seemed content to let me ask the questions. He rose a notch in my esteem. Sometimes Buck would call me in to ask questions when a female deputy wasn't available and a child was involved in a crime, either as a witness or a victim. That was how I knew what questions to ask. Of course, I always had Cisco with me at those times. That was the whole point. Because dogs make everything better.

Melanie took a sip of her juice, and Rita smoothed a tangled curl away from her granddaughter's face. She couldn't seem to stop touching Melanie; none of us could. Miles held her in the crook of his arm, Rita held her hand, I closed my fingers around her knee and smiled up at her. Home. Safe. But where was Cisco?

She said, "We came in from the beach after our walk. I started to take Cisco's leash off in the kitchen but he pulled away from me and ran toward the front door like there was someone there. I thought maybe you and Dad had come back early, so I came after him, but not very fast you know, because I didn't think anything was wrong, I just thought you were home. And when I got here there was a man standing over there..." she gestured toward the staircase area, "and he was feeding Cisco something."

My heart stopped. *Poison.* Cleaner and quieter than a gunshot, and the first thing a burglar would do if he was planning a big heist. Dispose of the family dog.

Somehow I managed an encouraging nod, but she must have seen my lips tremble because she rushed on, "So I yelled at him, I said 'Hey! What are you doing?' and I ran to get Cisco. Cisco kind of looked at me, and the man, he turned away from me real fast, like he was afraid I'd see his face, and then I knew for sure he was a bad guy. So I called to Cisco, I called 'Cisco, come!' just like you taught me, Raine, and he was going to do it, too, he started toward me, but then the guy stepped on his leash."

A big tear swam in her eye for a moment, then plopped on her cheek. "I should have taken his leash off. If I'd taken his leash off, he could've gotten away."

I said, in as strong a voice as I could possibly manage, "Melanie, this is not your fault. None of this is your fault. You did everything exactly right, okay? You did exactly what I would have done. This is not your fault."

Melanie looked at me with big wet eyes, and I knew she heard me, but she was a smart kid. That was what I loved about her. She was such a smart kid. She nodded, infinitesimally. I felt Miles's fingers cover mine, briefly, on Melanie's knee, and I could feel the tenderness in his eyes but I didn't dare look at him because if I did I wouldn't be able to go on. I said, "When the bad guy put his foot on Cisco's leash he must have turned around, right?"

She nodded. My heart speeded a little.

"And did you see his face then? Can you tell us what he looked like?"

She said, "He had something on his face. A stocking, I think. His face was all smushed down. Cisco didn't like it and he started barking. So I ran up to him and tried to grab Cisco's leash but that was when the bad guy grabbed me instead and put his hand over my mouth. I screamed and kicked and tried to bite him but I couldn't. Then he put this tape over my mouth, and tied my hands together with tape too. He was really strong. Then he put tape over my eyes too, and it really hurt later when I pulled it off because it was all tangled up in my hair." Gently, Rita stroked her hair, and I could see the reflexive pain cross her face. Melanie went on, "It all happened really fast, and Cisco was barking and jumping and I tried to kick but it didn't make any difference, he dragged me outside and then into this van, and Cisco too."

Oh God. Oh God, oh God. She had been kidnapped, she had come this close to being killed, because she had tried to save my dog. But she was Melanie. What else could she have done?

I had never loved anyone more in my life.

My own cheeks were wet, but if that was from tears, I ignored them. I said, "How do you know it was a van?"

She answered without hesitation, "I heard the doors slide. Just like the van that used to take us to after-school swimming and gymnastics back in New York." She paused and wrinkled her nose. "Only it smelled like garbage. And there weren't any seats."

"And he put Cisco in the van with you?"

She nodded. "He barked. And after a while when I was rolling around on the floor, you know, because there weren't any seatbelts, he came and he put his paws across my legs. I could hear him panting."

"But he was okay?" I had to ask. I had to. "He seemed okay to you?"

"He was Cisco," she said. "He took care of me."

I could feel my nose start to drip, and my chest go wet and heavy. I ignored it. I somehow found a smile. I squeezed Melanie's knee. "You're doing great, Mel. This is good intel, it's exactly what we need. Can you remember what happened next? Try to think about details. What you heard and smelled and felt."

I could see, from the corner of my eye, the inspector's surprised and appreciative glance. Miles stroked my arm. But for me, and perhaps for everyone else in the room, there was nothing but Melanie, and what she had to say.

She frowned thoughtfully. "We drove for a long time. Lots of turns. He put the radio on, but I could hear him talking to somebody. I think he was on the phone and he talked real low so I couldn't hear all the words, but he sounded mad. Or maybe scared."

"Do you think he was talking to somebody in the van? Before you said 'they'. Do you think someone was waiting for him in the van?"

Again she was thoughtful. "Maybe. I don't know. But later, after the van stopped and he got out, I only heard one door slam. And outside I could hear two people talking."

I prompted, "Could you hear anything they said?"

"I heard some bad words," she admitted. "And somebody said something about a felony, and about being careful. Or maybe not being careful. I don't know. I should have listened better."

"You did great," I assured her, squeezing her knee. I even managed a bracing smile. "Better than I would have done. Then what happened?"

"Then I heard the sliding door open again and Cisco…" She started to cry again, her face going wet and blotchy. "Cisco jumped out. I'm sorry, Raine, I would've caught him if I could but I couldn't!"

I wanted to spring up and hug her hard, but Miles beat me to it, turning his daughter into his arms and kissing her hair fiercely as he assured her, "This is not your fault. None of this is your fault, do you hear me?"

"Your dad is right," I added, though my voice was thick. "You are the smartest, bravest girl I've ever met and you did all the right things. And you know you don't have to worry about Cisco, don't you?" I even managed a smile. "He's a combination of Lassie, Rin Tin Tin and Super Man, all rolled into one. He's fine."

The sniffling slowed, and her grandmother handed her a tissue. "I could hear him barking when the van drove away," she said. "And after awhile I couldn't hear him anymore."

I nodded, trying to look encouraging, but all of a sudden I had lost my ability to speak. Miles took over for me.

"How did you get away, sweetheart?" he asked.

"I didn't." She sounded tired, as I could well imagine she was. "We drove some more, and then the van stopped and he pulled me out and cut off the tape on my hands and then he drove away, just like that, real fast. At first I was so scared, I couldn't even believe it, and I was crying so hard I could hardly breathe, so I took the tape off my mouth and then I got it off my eyes, and I was all alone on this strange road with no lights or anything. So then I started walking and I came to this one gate and pushed the buzzer but n-no one was home and finally I saw some lights but it took me a really long time to get to them because I kept going the wrong way, and I thought if Cisco had been there he could have found the way home…" She spoke to her lap, where she was shredding the damp tissue into a hundred little pieces. "But after awhile I realized that the lights I saw were from somebody's pool and then I knew where I was so I just kept walking until I saw our house."

I could hear Miles's breathing, slow and deep, from where I was. I did not have to look at his face to know what he was thinking. How easily it could have turned out differently. How many, many things could have gone wrong along the way. Rita said, "We're very glad you did, sweetheart. And Raine is right. You are the bravest, smartest little girl I have ever known."

Melanie looked at me with tears glittering in her eyes and she said, "But I couldn't save Cisco."

The inspector had a few more questions for Melanie: Would she recognize the street where she was released if she saw it again? Could she remember anything more at all about the van? But Miles put a stop to it before even five minutes had passed. Exhaustion, emotional and physical, was catching up with her, and there was relief in her face when she hugged her dad goodnight and went upstairs with Rita to prepare for bed.

"I believe, Mr. Young," said Inspector LeClerk when she was gone, "we are faced with two possibilities. The first is that your daughter interrupted a burglary in progress. As you look around, I take it you find nothing is missing?"

Miles gave an impatient shake of his head. He was pacing now, his hands shoved into his pockets, using up excess adrenaline now that the crisis was past. "I don't keep anything valuable here. I rent it out when I'm not using it. I'll ask my mother, but she doesn't usually travel with jewelry unless she's wearing it. Besides, that doesn't even make sense. Why break into a house while it's occupied when it sits empty for weeks on end?"

"And why take Melanie?" I asked. "And Cisco? Why not just run away?"

"Possibly because he was afraid she had seen him before he put his mask on. Possibly because she was making enough noise to attract attention, as was the dog. He may have only wanted to keep them quiet while he made his escape." A faint and sympathetic smile. "These behaviors are not always logical."

"You said there were two explanations," Miles said.

A small, very French shrug. "The second explanation is perhaps the easiest, but I would caution you the simplest explanation is not always the most accurate. It may well have been, as you suspected, an attempt at kidnapping, for ransom or other reasons. The kidnapper lost his nerve, or feared he had been seen, or for whatever reason decided the risk was too great. He fortunately was not prone to violence, and released your daughter unharmed."

"And the dog?" Miles said tightly.

"I suspect our criminal was unprepared to deal with a dog and, rather than allow him to continue to bark and draw attention, he secured him in the van. I will be very interested in where the animal eventually turns up, as it may well give us a clue as to where the child was taken which may, in turn, lead us to the kidnapper." He closed his notebook and stood. "I would of course like to talk to your daughter tomorrow after she has rested. No doubt we will gain new insights at that time. Should she happen to remember anything else before then, kindly telephone." He handed Miles a card. "And may I say how very pleased I am that this matter has come to such a happy conclusion. As you are no doubt aware, this is not always the case."

A bleakness came into Miles's eyes as the shadow of what had almost been crossed our path once more. He said simply, "Yes." He put the card into his pocket but did not offer his hand. "Good night Inspector. I need to be with my daughter now."

"Of course. Good night."

I walked Inspector LeClerk to the door. "Listen," I said, keeping my voice as steady as I could, "I know it doesn't seem important to you, but Cisco—my dog—he is important. He's not just a pet. I need you to help me find him. Please."

The inspector looked at me, and I thought I might have detected a trace of understanding in his eyes. "*Mais oui*, mademoiselle, I agree—this is no ordinary dog. He is evidence in a kidnapping, and you may be sure my officers will keep his description in mind. The outcome for Miss Young may be good, but this continues to be an open case."

I swallowed hard. Cisco was evidence in a kidnapping case. I hadn't thought of that. But I was pretty sure that, by now, the kidnappers had. And what do criminals do with evidence that could implicate them? Destroy it at the first opportunity.

I had to find him. I *had* to.

At the door the inspector paused, and looked back at me. "You have had experience with the police."

Somehow I managed to drag my thoughts away from the desperate path they had taken and back to the present. "Yes."

He nodded. "You should not think poorly of our small island for the attitude of the officer who first took your report about the missing child. The fact of the matter is he was correct— the majority of these events resolve themselves without intervention. That is not to say we do not take seriously the safety of every child who visits us here, but shall I tell you what first caused me to think there might be more to this situation than was apparent? It was when I heard your name."

I blinked. "What?"

"Yours and that of Mr. Young, of course," he went on. "An American actress perpetrates an elaborate hoax upon us all, and you are there. A boat burns at the marina, and you are there. Mere hours later a child is reported missing and you are there. It all seems very much a coincidence to me, Miss Stockton, and in police work..."

"There is no such thing as a coincidence," I murmured, because I had heard my uncle, my father and my ex-husband say it a thousand times. And I knew he was right. There were dots to be connected, of course there were, but try as I might I could not draw the lines. All I could think of was Cisco, alone and far from home, maybe wandering the busy streets of downtown Gustavia, maybe abandoned on the beach miles from here, maybe on a boat in the middle of the ocean, maybe none of those things at all. He was evidence in a kidnapping. Criminals disposed of evidence.

"*Exactement*." He smiled, and nodded politely to me. "Good night, mademoiselle. We'll talk again."

Cisco had been lost once before. A child had been missing then, too. It had been cold, and dark, and he had run off into the woods with a wild border collie who had later become one of his best friends. Of course everyone was Cisco's best friend. I had been on crutches at the time with a knee injury, and it was Maude who searched all night. Maude who knew how dogs think, the patterns in which they wander, where they are likely to go and what they are likely to avoid. Eventually Cisco and the border collie had been found, together, keeping the missing child warm in the woods. What would Maude have told me now? Where would she have had me look?

I missed her so much.

Once, when Miles and I were new acquaintances and I still was trying very hard not to like him, my collie Majesty escaped the house during a rainstorm and went missing all night. He had driven up and down muddy country roads looking for her, then had sat up with me all night while I checked the front porch and the back porch and the barn every fifteen minutes in case she had come home. That was when I first suspected he might be worth keeping.

Majesty had been found wet and muddy but otherwise unharmed, sitting on my aunt's front porch. Miles and I became friends, then more than friends. Because of that, I had met Melanie. And now Melanie had come home, safe and sound. There were happy endings. There *were*.

Then why couldn't I stop the panic from swelling up in my chest, building and building until it threatened to blow my world apart?

I stood on the balcony outside the French doors of Melanie's room, watching her asleep on her bed in Rita's arms. The ocean was loud below me, and the warm breeze tossed my hair around my face and neck. Inside, the room was dark but for the Little Mermaid nightlight, and Miles sat in a chair near the bed, watching her, too. All of us were keeping watch over one we loved. But one of those I loved was not there.

Eventually Miles noticed me, and got up. He kissed Melanie's forehead, and stood for another moment, looking down at her. Then he came out onto the balcony. I heard the door lock engage as he pulled it closed. In the time I had been here I don't think any of us had locked our doors at night. But I was glad to hear that sound now.

"Miles," I said with soft urgency as he came over to me, "I have to go look for Cisco. I can't just do nothing. You need to stay here with Melanie, but I have to go."

He put out a hand and caressed my shoulder gently. His face was weary and touched with regret, but his tone was firm. "Honey, I need you to stay here tonight; I can't let you leave."

I stepped away from his touch. Something about the way he used *I* twice in one sentence caused a flare of irrational anger within me. *I need. I can't.* What difference did it make what he needed? His baby was home. Mine was still missing.

"I don't need your permission," I said shortly, and turned on my heel to go. "I just wanted you to know."

He put his hand on my shoulder again, this time more firmly. "It's one in the morning," he said. "There's nothing you can do. And no one is leaving this house tonight."

I tried to pull away from him but he took my other shoulder and I turned on him, pushing hard against his chest. "I can't just leave him out there!" I cried. "He's lost and alone and he doesn't know how to find his way home! He's just a dog and he depends on me and…" Tears scalded my eyes and I looked at Miles, helpless to fight them. "I can't help him, can I? I don't know where to look. He's not on the beach. He's not in the neighborhood. They took him too far away. I don't know where to look. There's nothing I can do."

Miles started to say something about the morning but I didn't hear him. I couldn't hear him for the roaring in my ears, the black bubble of helpless pain that grew and grew until it suddenly burst in my chest and flooded my whole soul with big, ugly, shard-like sobs, the kind of sobs that suck the light out of the stars and the hope out of the universe. *There's nothing I can do* . The words kept playing over and over in my head, and for some reason so did pictures: my father, sitting on the edge of the bed after my mother's funeral, his face buried in her coat; Maude, taking a Christmas ham out of the oven; Cassidy, my first golden, breathing her last breath with her head in my lap; my husband and my best friend who promised to love me forever, looking at me with shame in his eyes as he betrayed our marriage for the last time. Pictures, pictures. Andy, who used to leave me graffiti love notes in the steam on the bathroom mirror when we lived together in college, walking into a rain of gunfire. My mother, pinning back my hair on my wedding day. Cisco, flying through the jumper's course, barreling through a locked screen door, carrying a basket of flowers at the senior center, scarfing down a whole platter of cookies five minutes later. Pictures, pictures, pictures.

Somehow I was on my knees, and Miles, sinking to the floor with me, wrapped his arms and his legs around me and pulled me close as though only by doing so could he keep the pieces of me from flying apart and being dispersed on the wind. I couldn't stop crying. I wanted to stop. I wanted to be strong for him, for Melanie, for Cisco, who needed me so much. But I couldn't stop until every bit of me was wrung out, dry, exhausted, empty. "I've lost so much," I whispered, my head against his chest, my fists bunched into his shirt. "I can't lose Cisco too. I just can't."

Miles took my hot, swollen face in his hands and tilted it to look up at him, wiping away the oozing tears with his thumbs. "You're not going to lose Cisco," he said. "And..." he pressed a long and tender kiss into my hair, "you're not going to lose me."

I said brokenly, "I don't believe you."

"Ah, baby." He laid my head against his shoulder, gently, and rested his chin atop my hair. "That's okay. Because I do."

CHAPTER TWELVE

I don't think I slept, but I must have dozed off and on throughout the endless night, because by the time I stepped out of the shower the next morning I was surprisingly clear-headed. It was as though the torrent of pain and defeat that had washed through me the night before had left me clean, lighter, ready to face whatever I had to face.

But I deliberately did not look at the empty designer dog bed with its small pile of toys when I passed.

The sky was a pale morning blue over the still ocean below, still streaked with pink in places, but Miles was already waiting for me on the balcony. His face showed the puffiness of sleeplessness and stress, but he, too, was freshly showered and changed. He handed me a cup of coffee when I came out. "No offense," I said as I accepted it, "but you look like hell."

"No offense back, but—"

"Don't say it."

He smiled tiredly and leaned against the rail.

I sipped my coffee. "Melanie is still sleeping?"

He nodded. "I've arranged for a plane to take Mom and her back home this morning."

I said, "I can't leave until I find Cisco. But you don't have to stay. You should be with Melanie."

A single dismissive shake of his head said that he had already considered the options, made up his mind, and moved on to other matters. "I printed out a bunch of fliers with Cisco's picture," he said. "Gustavia is the most likely place to start looking. We can blanket the town with fliers. The marina too. There are lots of Americans there this time of year, not the usual celebrity crowd. They like to sail down from Florida and Puerto Rico, and most of them are dog lovers."

I opened my mouth to thank him, but instead I said, "Felony." I frowned a little, puzzling over the memory. "Melanie said she heard the word 'felony'. As in 'kidnapping is a felony' which it is—in the United States. An American would say that. Maybe even an American who hasn't been here that long."

223

Something flickered across Miles's eyes, and he said, "Come inside for a minute."

I followed him the few steps across the balcony and to his room, hesitating just inside the door as he put his coffee cup on a table beside the sofa and proceeded across the room. There was a chrome-framed abstract painting on the wall, and he slid it to the right to reveal a small wall safe. He said, "Do you remember Melanie's birthday?"

"Yes, of course."

I watched him tap some numbers onto the keypad. "That's the code. Enter it twice. Month, day, year, then year, day, month."

"Miles, I'm not really comfortable …"

But I stopped speaking as he swung open the door. Inside was a 9 mm Glock, so stark and ugly on this gentle tropical morning that I actually caught my breath.

Miles took the pistol out of the safe and ejected the magazine, handling it with confidence and expertise. "Have you ever fired one of these?"

I nodded slowly. "Target practice."

"Fifteen rounds," he said, holding up the clip, "fully loaded and ready to fire." He snapped the magazine back into place and returned the gun to the safe.

"Miles, I don't think…" I began again, but I really didn't know how to finish.

"In the past twenty-four hours, my boat has been blown up, my security system tampered with, and my child kidnapped," he said shortly. "You need to know where the damn gun is."

In a moment I nodded. He was right. I did. "I don't like it when I don't know what you're thinking."

He looked at me steadily. "You know exactly what I'm thinking."

I drew in a slow breath. "So," I said, "about how much money would Alex Barry need to shore up his company, anyway?"

Miles picked up his coffee again. "More than I have, at least in ready cash. That's the only thing that doesn't make sense about the kidnapping scenario."

"That and the fact that he was with us the entire time this was going on."

"Possibly so he would have an airtight alibi. But he's involved in this somehow. What I have to do is figure out how."

I said cautiously, "And then?"

There was a hard glint in Miles's eyes I had never seen before, and it gave me a chill. "That," he replied, "depends entirely on what I find out."

I thought about it for only a moment. "So," I said. "When are we going to go talk to him?"

He looked for a moment as though he might argue with me, then recognized it would only be a waste of time. "It means putting off the search for Cisco," he warned.

I answered, "But it might be our best chance of finding him."

Miles nodded, "I think so too." He glanced at his watch. "They've scheduled that press conference for eight this morning. I think they're trying to make the morning news shows. I doubt if we'd be disturbing anyone if we showed up now, but I need to tell Mom we're leaving."

Rita, who was making waffles for a still sleeping Melanie when we came down, was not at all pleased when Miles told her his plans—not the ones about confronting Alex, but the ones about sending Melanie and her home.

"Miles," she said, putting down the whisk with which she had been beating several eggs into an unnecessary submission, "I know she's your daughter and you have to do what you think is best, but are you sure about this? You didn't want her to be afraid of the water, but if you send her home now don't you think you run the risk of making her afraid of everything?"

Miles gave a sharp shake of his head, brows drawing together. "That's not the point. She isn't safe here. Maybe she does need to be a little afraid."

Privately, I agreed with Rita, but I tried a different approach. "Have the police even cleared her to leave? She's a witness to a crime."

"I haven't checked with the police. They have her statement."

This was the stubborn side of Miles I knew too well and had not yet learned how to manage. I looked helplessly at Rita, but she just leaned against the countertop and looked helplessly back at me.

"Dad?" Melanie stood at the doorway in shortie pajamas with multicolored paw prints printed all over them, looking rumpled and tousled and sleep-fresh, but also a little worried. "We're not going home without Cisco, are we?"

Miles went over to her, picked her up, and kissed her soundly. "Do you know how good you look to me this morning?"

She wriggled to be put down, and since she was barely a foot shorter than I was, it wasn't much of a struggle. "What about Cisco?" she demanded.

"We're not leaving without Cisco," I assured her.

"But I think your grandmother and you should go home early," Miles said. "Raine and I are going to stay here until we find him."

She looked at her father with a kind of helpless disbelief. "I can't leave without Cisco," she said. "I'm the one that lost him!"

"No," I said quickly. "Melanie, you didn't lose him. You and Cisco were both lost together, you just came home first, that's all."

But this time, in the bright light of day with all the nightmares behind her, it didn't work. "Dad," she pleaded, "don't make me go home without him!"

I saw in her eyes a very familiar desperation; it was the same kind of helplessness I had felt last night. I turned my back on Melanie and spoke very quietly to Miles. He would only get one shot at getting this right "Miles," I said, "don't take her power away."

Rita stepped forward and touched his arm. "Maybe you should listen to Raine, Miles. It would only be for another day or two."

He looked from his mother to me as though he wanted to understand,   and usually he did understand, but this time he was a man trying to protect his family in the only way he knew how and he just didn't get it.   He said to Melanie, "Sweetheart, I'm sorry but—"

In the other room, the phone rang, and we all froze. It was seven-thirty in the morning, and the sound was like an alarm bell. Miles went quickly to answer it, and none of us was far behind.

Miles spoke tensely into the receiver and then glanced at us. "It's the police," he said. I moved closer. He listened for another minute, and I saw the relief wash over his face. "Thank God," he said. He stretched out a hand to me.

I whispered, "Cisco?"

Miles nodded, and covered the receiver with his hand. "He's okay," he said. "They found him."

Melanie flung herself on me, grinning from ear to ear, and I hugged her hard, too weak and too relieved to speak. I could barely draw a breath. I heard Miles say, "Okay, we'll be there in fifteen minutes. Thank you, Inspector."

Miles hung up the phone and I managed, "Where?" My voice sounded strained and I think I was shaking a little—okay a lot—as my heart kicked into high gear and the adrenaline of relief surged through me, turning my muscles to jelly.

"The marina," Miles said. "Apparently he was being kept on a boat."

"I'll get dressed!" Melanie cried, but Miles caught her hand before she could race off.

"Whoa, there, cowgirl," he said. "You need to stay home with Grandma on this trip. We'll deliver Cisco right to your door."

Melanie looked devastated, and, as anxious as I was to get to Cisco, I thought he was being unnecessarily harsh. But it was Rita who said, "Miles, don't you think—?"

He gave a small shake of his head, and his expression went grim. "The news is not all good," he said. "The place they found Cisco is a crime scene now." He drew Melanie to him in a gesture of comfort and reassurance as he added, "A man is dead, and they think it's the kidnapper."

Crime investigation among the uber rich and famous, I was beginning to understand, was conducted very discretely in this island sanctuary. The Port of Gustavia, home to some of the most luxurious yachts in the world, would not be inconvenienced by something so gauche as a death onboard one of its lesser vessels. There was no police tape, no security check, no emergency vehicles with flashing lights. Things were very, very different here.

We parked near the deep-water area of the marina, and I was glad not to have to walk past the charred skeleton of Miles's sailboat with all the horrifying memories of the night before. I knew, of course, that the remains of that sailboat might well end up being part of the story that had led to

Melanie's and Cisco's kidnapping, but at that moment I was not interested in the story. All I wanted to know was where my dog was.

Inspector LeClerk met us on the dock, and those were my first words as I rushed toward him. "Where is he?" I demanded. "Where is Cisco? You didn't put him in a police car in this heat, did you? You didn't leave him alone on the boat?"

The inspector held up a staying hand. "Your dog is quite well, mademoiselle. He is being held in the office of the harbor master. I will escort you." I turned in that direction without waiting for his "escort." But I could hear the trace of a smile in his voice as he added, "He is quite a—how shall we say?—handful, this Cisco of yours."

Miles walked on the other side of me, fingers brushing mine. "How did you find him?"

"Apparently some of the overnight guests on neighboring yachts were disturbed by the persistent barking throughout the night. When an employee of the marina went onboard to investigate, they found the dog tied up inside the wheelhouse..."

I winced at the thought, and walked faster. Cisco hated to be confined. No wonder he had barked.

"And what was assumed to be his owner in the cabin below, dead of an apparent combination of alcohol and amphetamines which may have been accidental, or perhaps intentional. When the investigating officers arrived they recognized the description of the breed, and of course the US identification tags." The smile this time was accompanied by a small tilt of his head toward me. "You recall, mademoiselle, I assured you my officers were well aware of the importance of locating the animal. And so they have."

I nodded impatiently, turning down the walkway toward the big, glass and stone structure that welcomed yachtsmen to Gustavia Harbor. "Yes." And then I remembered to add, "Thank you."

Miles said, "Whose yacht was it?"

"The boat was one of a small fleet of excursion craft registered to Evergreen Concierge."

I slowed down, and Miles and I looked at each other. It was starting to make sense. I said, "Didn't your mom say that the concierge service was delivering dinner last night?"

"They cater parties, private dinners, even pick up and deliver meals from restaurants in town," Miles replied, his thoughts tracking with mine. "No one would even notice one of their vans on the street, or in the driveway of a villa."

"The van," I said. "Melanie said it smelled like garbage. An empty catering van might smell of old food and dirty dishes. And it wouldn't have seats."

"And Evergreen catered dinner on the boat last night."

The inspector looked at us with interest. "An interesting theory, and one we are already investigating. The dead man appears to be an employee of Evergreen, according to his identification." He consulted his notes. "His name was Richard Chambliss. A Canadian."

I stopped walking, even though the door that led to Cisco was only a few dozen steps away. My skin prickled in the bright morning sun. "Rick," I said, stunned.

Miles was not as fast to catch on as I was so I explained, "We met him on the beach. He was at the house yesterday." And then I felt a catch in my heartbeat. "Of course," I breathed, placing my hand on Miles's arm. "Melanie told him they were going to the beach after dinner. He would have known exactly what time their dinner was delivered."

"He could have disabled the cameras when he was at the house," Miles said. "That's probably why he came."

"He would have been waiting in the house for her while they were at the beach..."

"Evergreen has a passkey," Miles said tightly. "That's how the cleaning service gets in."

"And the guy who sets up the dog beds," I said, almost in a whisper.

Suddenly I couldn't wait another moment to see Cisco. I practically ran the next few steps and pushed open the glass door to the busy, light-filled building before either of the men could do it for me. I stood for a moment, getting my bearings—a view of the glistening blue harbor from every window, televisions on every wall tuned to news and weather, maps and signs in French and English— before spotting the circular marble desk and the crowd surrounding it. I started toward it, but the inspector raised a hand. "Mademoiselle will permit me?"

I waited impatiently as he went behind the desk and spoke to a young woman in a sleeveless white blouse and a pencil skirt, who glanced at us, nodded, and departed down a hallway. I listened for the sound of barking, but it was too noisy inside the big, echoing building to hear anything.

I said to Miles, "The hotdogs. Remember, I found a package of hotdog treats the other night when the lights went out? I thought I had dropped them when we came back from the beach, but I'd told Rick about using microwave-dehydrated hotdog slices to train dogs... I think he was trying to get into the house that night, and he brought the treats to distract Cisco. That's what he was probably feeding him last night when Melanie came in, too."

Miles said, "Damn it." through tightly gritted teeth. "You said someone pushed you. I should have looked harder."

"It wasn't your fault," I said. "We both thought it was the bird Cisco was barking at."

One of the television screens caught my eye, and I drew Miles's attention to it. The caption said, "Actress Returns From the Dead", and there was Rachelle Denison wearing a coral sundress and flawless makeup, glossy hair tied back with a white chiffon scarf whose ends floated in the sea breeze like delicate wings. She stood in the colorful tropical garden of what I assumed to be her St. Bart's home, her loving husband by her side and Cocoa gazing up at her adoringly, clearly glad to have everything right in his world again. I felt a little stab of sadness when I remembered Rick telling us how crazy Rachelle and Cocoa were about each other, not because I in anyway felt sorry for Rick—or Rachelle, for that matter—but because Rick had seemed like a nice guy and a dog lover, and now he was dead.

"He certainly has changed his tune," Miles muttered.

I realized he was referring to Alex, who drew his wife into a smiling, affectionate one-armed embrace, said something to the camera, and kissed her tenderly. Cut to the morning news anchor while

B-roll played in the background of Rachelle dropping to her knees with open arms to greet the enthusiastic doggie kisses of her wriggling golden retriever. It was the kind of footage designed to go viral, but what else could you expect from an actress who staged her own death to promote a movie? These people were pros.

The inspector was on the phone as he returned to us, speaking in terse, rapid French. He pocketed the phone and said to Miles, "We have received more information about this Richard Chambliss. It would appear his Canadian passport is false, and he has a criminal record in the states. We will of course ask your daughter to look at some photographs for identification purposes—"

Miles said harshly, "My daughter is not looking at crime scene photos. That's out of the question."

From what I knew of Melanie she would be unfazed, and had most likely seen worse things on HBO. But fathers, especially those who are still uncertain about their parenting skills, prefer to deceive themselves about some things, and I supposed he was entitled. I pointed out in his defense, "She already knew Rick, so a positive ID wouldn't be much help. And she didn't see his face last night."

The inspector nodded. "This I understand. It is procedure. We would naturally employ only photographs that depict the victim in the bloom of health. I imagine the American prison system could provide us with those."

A second television screen, this one captioned in French, was playing the footage of Cocoa greeting his long lost mistress while she laughed and embraced him. Apparently her publicity manager was working overtime. I turned impatiently to the inspector to demand the whereabouts of my own dog, and then every muscle in my body sagged with relief. There he was, huffing like a freight train at the end of his leash, dragging the rather alarmed-looking young woman in the pencil skirt behind him like a skier. He was already pulling so hard that his feet were going crooked and the woman on the other end of the leash was in genuine danger of losing whatever precarious balance she might have in the high heels, but I couldn't help myself. I dropped to my knees, flung open my arms, and cried, "Cisco!"

That was all it took. With one mighty lunge, he pulled the leash from his hapless handler's hand and galloped toward me, tongue lolling, claws scrambling and slipping on the floor. I knew at that speed he would knock me down if I allowed him to leap into my arms as I'd intended, so I got quickly into obedience stance, planted my feet, and called clearly, "Cisco, halt!"

He hit my knees so hard that, had not Miles been close enough to catch me, my feet would have gone flying out from under me. He barreled right past me and I swung around in horror to watch the path of destruction he plowed through the crowd. People swore in French and English, some of them laughed, others squealed and shrank back. I didn't bother calling him again. My dog training instincts kicked in and I yelled from the depths of my diaphragm, "*Hey!*". My voice boomed across the room, and it was just enough to make his head swivel toward me. When it did I tossed a training treat and hit him on the nose. As he snuffled to find the treat and gobble it up, I managed to close enough distance between us to grab his leash, tossing treats all the while.

Holding the leash with both hands, I brought the reluctant golden retriever back over to the two men. "And so, mademoiselle," the inspector said with a smirk that was both amused and annoyed, "a happy reunion."

I looked at Miles with all the helplessness and despair I felt inside bubbling to my eyes. He already knew what I was going to say. "This is not Cisco."

The inspector objected, "But his identification…"

I gave a short, broken-hearted shake of my head. "He switched the collars. This is not my dog."

Miles shifted his frowning gaze from me to the television on the wall. Even though nothing was on the screen now except a commercial, I saw confusion turn to understanding in his eyes, and a half-second later, I got it too.

The dog, Alex Barry had said last night. *He didn't come home.* Yet only moments ago the entire world had seen Rachelle Barry's dog happily running into her arms.

Miles's expression was grim. "It was never Melanie they were after," he said. "It was Cisco."

CHAPTER THIRTEEN

Golden retrievers are almost indiscriminately affectionate dogs who, if properly socialized and trained, genuinely want to please the humans who feed and shelter them. This is why goldens make such great service dogs and canine actors: they can easily transfer their obedience between one handler and another. Does this make them disloyal? Of course not. It makes them adaptable. Almost any golden retriever could have played the role of Rachelle Barry's adoring pet, as long as she showered him with treats and affection. But only one who was a dead ringer for Cocoa could have fooled his own family.

The question, of course, was why. And there was really only one answer.

There were still a few paparazzi lingering outside of Alex Barry's gate when we were buzzed through, and a couple of them snapped our picture just in case we were anyone important. I hoped they got a good shot of Cocoa, who was barking and bouncing from window to window in the back of the car.

A security guard met us at the door and escorted us around the house via a columned marble lanai that overlooked a series of velvet green terraces leading to the beach. On one of those terraces, photographer's screens and light reflectors had been set up, and Rachelle Denison posed for more photos with her loving golden retriever. *Get your hands off my dog, bitch!* I wanted to scream down at her, and then I wanted to run and grab Cisco and let the chips fall as they may, but Miles's light touch on my arm reminded me of our deal. He would not punch Alex Barry in the teeth, and I would not pull out Rachelle Denison's hair. At least not right away.

Besides, I had my hands full with her dog who, now that he was on familiar ground—or possibly because he smelled Cisco—showed signs of losing interest in the treats that had kept him by my side thus far, and threatened to make a break for it at the first possible opportunity.

Evidence of the press conference was still in view on the tiled patio as we reached it—the elaborate chrome and steel outdoor kitchen set-up with urns of coffee and a buffet of pastries and fruit platters, a few stray extension cords, some folding chairs stacked against a wall. Alex, who had apparently just been notified of our arrival, came out of the house through the open glass doors, but Susan was already there. She rushed toward Miles when she saw him, sweeping him into an embrace.

"Oh, Miles, I just heard about your boat! What an awful thing! But I'm so glad you weren't hurt."

Miles received her affection without reciprocation, his face like granite. He took her arms and stepped away, but not before I saw her eyes flicker over his shoulder from Cocoa to the place where Rachelle was posing with the fake Cocoa, and there definitely was a shadow of confusion there—along with what very well might have been alarm. It was quickly gone, though, as she looked up at Miles with a sympathetic smile and added, "I know how crazy you were about that boat."

"I was," he admitted, his voice cold. "But I'm even crazier about my daughter."

She managed to look confused, even slightly hurt, but once again the dart of a glance toward Cocoa, who was nibbling a treat from my fingers so aggressively that he threatened to take skin, betrayed her.

Alex came toward Miles with his hand extended. "Miles, I just heard from the office what happened last night. I know how upsetting this must be for you. We need to sit down and talk."

Miles ignored his hand. "We definitely need to talk."

Alex rubbed his hands together nervously, then gestured toward the buffet. "Let me get you some coffee. It's been a crazy couple of days for both of us."

Miles said, "Well, let's see. You've lost a wife and had her come back from the dead. My boat has been blown up, my house broken into, my daughter taken—"

"And my dog," I put in.

"Yes," Miles concluded, "a crazy couple of days."

Susan looked distressed. "Your daughter? But—she's okay, isn't she? You got her back?" She glanced again at Cocoa, and at me. "I mean, you got your dog back."

"Yes," Miles said. "We found them both, unharmed."

Alex returned from the buffet with two cups of coffee, looking somewhat less agitated now. He offered one to me and I shook my head. When he offered a cup to Miles, he ignored him. "I want you to know I've got my best men working on trying to figure out what happened to the cameras," he said, setting the coffee on a table. "But my advice to you is to look into hiring personal security. These are dangerous times we live in."

The man was brazen. I shifted a quick glance to Miles, but I needn't have worried. "Aren't they just?" he agreed with a thoughtful nod. "But save yourself some man hours, Alex. I already know what happened to the cameras."

Alex sank down onto the plushly cushioned wicker settee and stretched one arm across the back, looking interested and relaxed. "Oh?"

"They were disabled," Miles said, "by one of your employees."

Alex sat up straight. "Now wait just a minute."

On the terrace below, the photo session had ended. The photographer packed up his equipment while Rachelle chatted with him. She wasn't even holding Cisco's leash. Was she crazy? Clearly she knew nothing about dogs. I wanted to drop Cocoa's leash and run to Cisco, to wrestle the other woman to the ground if I had to, and bring him to safety. I had to grind my teeth together to keep from calling him. *Not yet, not yet.* Not until he was close enough for me to touch. I dug in my pocket for another treat for Cocoa.

"It's all right," Miles said. He watched Alex; I watched Susan. "The police caught the guy."

"Thank goodness," said Susan. Her fingers fluttered around a thin gold necklace she wore at her throat. But her eyes were watching Rachelle and Cisco.

"His name was Rick Chambliss," Miles said. "I'm sure you remember him. You mentioned him at lunch."

Alex frowned. "The dog guy?" He seemed genuinely perplexed. "He's the one who broke into your house?"

"And kidnapped my child," Miles reminded him.

"And my dog," I said. I did not take my gaze off Susan.

"That," said Alex, still frowning, "is very bad news."

"Even worse for Rick," I said. "He's dead. An apparent overdose of amphetamines and alcohol."

"Amphetamines," Miles repeated pointedly. "Aren't they sometimes used in prescription diet pills?"

"Like the ones your wife took before she went diving and drowned," I said. "I mean, almost drowned. Weird coincidence. She mixed them with alcohol too."

"The police will probably want to talk to her about that," Miles said.

"Good God, Miles," Susan said sharply, "you can't seriously mean to imply that Rachelle had anything to do with that boy's death! Certainly not with what happened to your little girl!"

But Alex just sat there, staring at Miles, until Rachelle and Cisco started up the steps to the patio. Then he moved his eyes slowly to Rachelle.

I said, "I'm pretty sure Rachelle didn't have anything to do with either one, since she has been dead for two days."

Now Alex looked at me, sharply. Miles spoke before he could.

"The thing I couldn't figure out," Miles said to Alex, "was how you did it by yourself. There were divers all over that reef after you sounded the alarm, and plenty of witnesses. The success of your whole plan depended on none of them finding the body. Where would you have hidden it until you had a chance to dispose of it? You had to have help."

Now his gaze moved to Susan. "You don't dive," he said, "but you're a good sailor. I taught you myself. My guess is that you were on one of those boats that night, but instead of aiding with the search, you were hiding Rachelle's body onboard."

Her eyes went wide with something that was halfway between incredulity and a kind of forced amusement. "Oh, for God's sake, Miles, are you serious? In the first place, I can't believe you would think—much less say!—that I would do something like that! In the second place..." Her laugh was too dry and her gesture too big. "Rachelle is very much alive! You saw her yourself yesterday, and the whole world saw her on television this morning, and if you don't believe me, ask her yourself!"

"I'd rather ask Alex," said Miles, "who was just drunk enough last night to tell us the truth. That woman is not Rachelle Denison."

Susan just laughed again. "Since when do you believe anything my brother says? Particularly when he's drunk!"

Alex said nothing. He just watched Rachelle and Cisco come up the steps, and so did I. *Come on, Cisco, come on. Just a little farther.*

But I made myself look away, and say in as conversational a tone as I could manage, "He also mentioned yesterday that you were the one who introduced Rachelle to her understudy—or body double, as they call them in the movies— and I'm guessing that's who was at the airport the day we came in. She was wearing a white chiffon scarf to hide her face and she was in such a hurry to get out of there she dropped her boarding pass—to the ferry."

"She probably flew commercial into St. Martin," supplied Miles, "and took the ferry over to avoid the record of a private flight into St. Bart's. Then, just to make sure she covered her tracks, she took a cab to the airport, where drivers are accustomed to picking up incognito guests and no one asks any questions."

Susan gave an amused shake of her head. "Miles, you're astonishing. Who knew you had such an imagination? If you'd used some of it while we were married, we might have lasted longer."

"I doubt that," replied Miles. He sounded a little sad. "If I had used any imagination at all, I would have known what you were a lot sooner."

The amusement faded from her face.

I said, "She would have had to have been a pretty close look-alike to step in for Rachelle in some of those action scenes. Directors like close-ups these days, they're more convincing. With hair and make-up, a really good actress could fool just about anyone. Except her dog."

"Now I see where this is coming from." Susan's cool smile did not touch her eyes as she looked at Miles. "Congratulations, darling, you finally found someone as impressionable as you are."

Alex turned his head slowly to look at Susan. "My God," he said quietly. I couldn't tell whether the expression in his tone was contempt or admiration. "You did this? All of it?"

Susan shot him an annoyed look. "Shut up, Alex. They're trying to trap you into saying something, God knows why. The whole thing is some absurd little drama the two of them have concocted and they're so pathetic they don't realize it doesn't even make sense. Even if it were possible to kill a person and bring someone else in to take her place, why *would* you, for heaven's sake? And to think you could get away with impersonating someone as famous as Rachelle Denison? It's ridiculous."

"But that's what made it easy," I said. "Rachelle wasn't that famous. Not like a major movie star with hundreds of handlers, advisors and hangers-on, not to mention fans, that you'd have to fool. She had just been in the business a few years, didn't have that many friends, no close relatives. Her show had been canceled for almost a year, so she didn't go to work every day. Her agent, her manager, her lawyer—those were the only people you really had to worry about fooling. And you didn't even have to fool them for very long—just until today, when Rachelle turned thirty and came into full control of her trust. The only problem was that everyone—and I mean *everyone*—knew how crazy she was about Cocoa, and how she was the only one who could control him. The first time Cocoa ran past her without recognizing her, or ignored her command, the gig would be up. So your first thought was to get rid of Cocoa. But you forgot to tell Rachelle—the fake Rachelle—you had done that, so when I asked her about Cocoa yesterday she told everyone in the room how happy Cocoa had been to see her when she got home. Big mistake, since she'd just blown your excuse for why Cocoa couldn't be in all the photos with her, like he always was. "

My throat contracted a little at the realization that I, with my careless interference, had been the cause of Cisco's kidnapping, and Melanie's. But I pushed determinedly on. "You had already seen how much Cisco looked like Cocoa, and how well-trained he was, and you figured that if you could pass off an imposter as Rachelle you could definitely pass Cisco off as her dog. But something went wrong, didn't it? Melanie got in the way."

"Oh, for heaven's sake." Susan turned impatiently on her heel toward the house. "I don't have to listen to this. Show them out, will you Alex?"

But Alex's eyes, and mine, were on Rachelle and Cisco. They had almost reached us, but Cisco hadn't seen me yet, and the sea breeze had kept him from sniffing out Cocoa. The fake Rachelle, looking movie-star perfect in her wind-tossed coral dress and chiffon scarf, raised her hand to wave at us, and that's when it happened. Cisco's head swiveled and his ears went forward. I knew exactly what was going to happen next, although I did not immediately know the reason why. Part of me thought, *No, no, no...* while another part thought, *Run, Cisco, run, run as fast as you can!*

And that was exactly what he did. Rachelle was barely holding the leash at all and she gave a startled little cry as he jerked it out of her hand on his way back down the terraces to the beach. He galloped past the photographer, who didn't even try to stop him. He galloped toward the sound of a voice he loved, and my heart stopped as I recognized it too.

My eyes flew to Miles in a flash of panic and he started forward, but Melanie was too fast for us. Rachelle, remembering herself, cried, "Cocoa, Cocoa, you bad dog, come here!" almost at the same moment as Melanie came running up the terrace steps from the beach, a delighted Cisco bouncing at her side. "It's okay, lady, I've got him!" she called.

We had had such a great plan, Miles and I. Not a perfect plan, to be sure, but one that was as foolproof as we could possibly make it. We had not counted on this. How could we? It all spiraled out of our control within seconds, and there was absolutely nothing we could do.

Rachelle turned to thank Melanie and to take Cisco's leash. Rita came up the steps only a moment behind Melanie, wearing her sun hat and carrying a beach bag over her shoulder, exclaiming, "I'm so sorry! Melanie you can't just run off like that!"

It was easy to see what had happened. Melanie, too excited about Cisco's safe return to stay still and with only a few hours left in the islands, had become impossible to keep in the house. Rita had agreed to let her go down to the beach while waiting for us to return, fully confident that the danger had passed. The kidnapper was dead, Cisco was on his way home, and she would not allow her grandchild to live in fear. The Barry estate was less than a five-minute walk up the beach. Why shouldn't Melanie have called out a greeting to Cocoa when she saw him on the terrace above? And why shouldn't Cisco, hearing her voice, have run toward her?

Still, everything might have been fine if Melanie had simply returned the leash to Rachelle and raced back down the hill, or if Rita had had time to catch up with her. But before either of those things could happen, Melanie noticed us.

"Dad!" she exclaimed. And then, seeing me standing there holding Cocoa's leash, her face split into a wide, delighted grin and she cried, "Cisco!" she thrust the leash she was holding into Rachelle's hand and raced toward us.

Cisco naturally noticed us as well and raced after her. Rachelle either never had a good grip on the leash at all, or dropped it in surprise. Cocoa, seeing both a child and a loose dog running toward him, lunged forward. I did the only thing I could think to do. I dropped the leash.

Cocoa, doubtless remembering their last romp on the beach, plowed happily into Cisco and the two dogs rolled and tumbled across the grass, red leashes tangling, until even I lost sight of which one was Cisco. Rachelle, directly in their path, cried out and shrank back, and Rita held onto the rail. The confusion gave Miles a chance to run forward and scoop up an astonished Melanie, which was all I had wanted.

Cisco and Cocoa regained their feet and started racing in happy circles, tails whirling, faces grinning, cutting and bowing, spinning and dashing. As far as Cisco was concerned, his family was back together, no one had given him a counter-command, and it was time to party. As for Cocoa, he had never missed a chance to run wild and he wasn't about to begin now. A stack of chairs went flying. An urn filled with cut flowers tumbled to the ground. One of the leashes caught the leg of a glass table and sent it crashing to the stone patio. Susan cried out, "For God's sake, Lisa, catch him!"

Rachelle shrank back in dismay. "Which one?"

And I think we all realized what Susan had said at the same moment.

My uncle, sheriff for thirty years, used to say that crimes usually are not committed by smart people. Most of the time this is true. But this particular crime, this elaborate production of a hoax, was a very smart crime, committed by a very smart person. I spent a lot of time afterwards trying to figure out how someone who had planned everything down to the smallest detail, even going so far as to kidnap a golden retriever to make sure the imposter was photographed with her beloved pet, could have made such a stupid, careless mistake. And then it occurred to me. Susan was the producer, not the talent. She was not prepared to step into a major role in her own play. She was, quite simply, under-rehearsed.

Alex stood slowly, staring at Susan. "Jesus Christ," he said. Again, it would have been impossible to say with any degree of accuracy whether his expression was disbelief or admiration, or perhaps a mixture of both.

The dog game had circled toward me, and I ran forward and grabbed one of the leashes, leaving Rachelle to snatch up the other. I honestly did not know until the leash was in my hand which golden retriever I had. And I was sure Rachelle did not.

Miles set Melanie on her feet and pushed her into Rita's arms. "Get her out of here," he commanded.

Rita wrapped both arms around Melanie's chest and took a backward step down the stairs. That was when Susan said, "Stop right there." And Rita's eyes went wide. She stopped.

I turned, and saw Susan standing on the patio with a gun in her hand.

I don't know where she got it. It was the kind of powerful, compact weapon a man obsessed with security would have kept stashed strategically around his house in easy-to-reach places. Perhaps in a kitchen drawer just inside the open door. Perhaps in a hidden compartment underneath the outdoor bar. Perhaps in a flower urn. She held the weapon in a strong, two-handed grip, and it was pointed at Melanie.

Miles stepped in front of his daughter. I felt my breath go still.

"Okay, Susan," he said calmly, "that's enough. You were the one who was concerned about a felony kidnapping. You're not going to shoot anybody. Why don't you just put the gun down before this gets out of hand?"

Her gaze was steady, and so was her aim, for a long and terrifying moment. She said, without shifting the gun, "I'm sorry about your boat, Miles. It was supposed to be a distraction, not a total loss. And I never meant to hurt your little girl. God, I'm not a monster. And you were always good to me. But Rick... what an idiot. The only thing he got right was getting Rachelle's body in the boat that night and dumping it out at sea. After that, it was one giant screw-up after another."

I looked desperately back down toward the terrace, where the photographer who had been left behind might be our only hope. If he came in sight of the patio and saw a woman with a gun... But he had moved his equipment down to the beach and was setting up for shots of the ocean. He was not coming back to the house.

I wound the leash around my hand twice for security, and I spoke up solely to get her attention away from Miles. My voice was a little shaky, I won't deny. "You knew Rick had a criminal record, and used it against him. Is that how you got him to work for you?"

She cast me a dismissive glance. "I'm the one who got him this job. He was small-time, B&E, and most of what he scored went up his nose. This should have been a simple in-and-out, the easiest job he'd ever done. But he couldn't get rid of the damn dog. That was all I asked him to do. Get rid of the dog. And then twice—*twice*—he bungled the break-in. All he had to do was put a leash on a *dog* , for God's sake. Some people are too stupid to live."

"So you killed him," Miles said.

She shrugged. "He was a liability. Sentimental, stupid, and a coke-head—not to mention that he knew way, way too much. He was completely unreliable. He would have overdosed himself eventually. I just hurried it along."

My friend, Sonny, believes that dogs can read our minds, and sometimes she has actually seemed to be able to communicate with them. I am skeptical, but before an agility run I will often picture the course in my head and whisper the commands to Cisco as though he could remember them. And what handler hasn't stood across from her dog during the long down in an obedience trial thinking *Stay, stay, stay…*? It was for all of these reasons that I studiously kept my eyes off my dog, that I deliberately did not think about him at all, even though my heart was bursting in my chest to have him so close and still in danger. I did not want to take the slightest chance that he would read something in my body language, or my mind, that would draw attention to himself and upset the delicate balance of power between the crazy person who held the gun and all the rest of us.

So I deliberately kept my focus on anything other than my dog, and the terribly vulnerable position he was in. I said, "What I don't understand is why you came to Miles. You had everything under control. All you had to do was keep people believing Rachelle was alive for another few hours and then you and Alex would have control of her fortune. Why risk everything by bringing someone else in?"

She cast a single, contemptuous glance at me. "So you're not as smart as I thought. I couldn't let Alex in on this. He was too greedy. And I hate to admit it, but a little smarter than I thought. He almost ruined everything at the press conference yesterday. And here's the funny thing— it was the dog that made him think he might have been wrong the first time, and this might really be Rachelle. That's how they all looked like such a happy family on television this morning. You're right— everybody knew about Rachelle and that damn dog." She cast a brief glance in the direction of Alex, who was standing near her right shoulder, but never really took   her attention, or the gun, off Miles. She said, "But letting Alex sit in jail while prosecutors and defense lawyers dug around for evidence wasn't an option. We had to have him where we could control him."

"Or dispose of him," said Miles. He kept his gaze, very calm, very neutral, on Susan, and on Alex behind her. I tried very hard not to look at anything at all.

Susan just smiled. "In a situation like this, it's important to be prepared for any contingency. It would have been better if the police hadn't tried to get cute at all. The only point of planting the regulator was to make sure that if anyone, including Alex, decided to claim that Rachelle was really dead, it would look as though he killed her. But when he got scared and called that press conference, we had to do our big reveal before we were ready." She shrugged. "We knew things might not go according to plan, and we had a Plan B. Fortunately, we also have a Plan C."

Rachelle, whose name was actually Lisa, said impatiently, "What am I supposed to do with this dog now? Can't I just let him go?"

"No," Lisa said sharply. "Bring him over here." To Miles she said, "You're right. I'm not going to shoot anyone. A little girl, a grandmother... That's just not me. But I'll kill both of these dogs right in front of your kid and it won't cause me a minute's pain. I don't even like dogs."

Looking at her, I knew she would do it, and my heart contracted in my chest. I wound the leash tighter in my hand. I did not look at my dog.

Melanie said in a small, tight voice, "Daddy, don't let her hurt the dogs. Don't let her shoot Cisco." And I could see, from my position, Rita's arms tighten around Melanie. Miles kept his eyes on Susan.

He said, "You've got to know this isn't going to work. Too many people know the truth now. Do you really think you can keep all of us quiet? There are too many loose ends. What if the police find Rachelle's body? And what about your patsy here…" He glanced at the woman playing the part of Rachelle. "Lisa, is it? As soon as she gets her hands on the trust fund she won't need you anymore. You haven't thought this through."

Lisa laughed and glanced at Susan. Susan just smiled. Lisa said, "Men are so naïve. Susan and I were together long before we came up with this plan. In fact, the whole thing was actually my idea, two years ago, when Rachelle got the stomach flu and Susan called me in to do a television interview for her. No one even knew it was me! I already knew I was a better actress than she was, but that day proved I could even be a better *Rachelle* than she was. So Susan and I started planning, and rehearsing, and getting everything just right for the day we'd start our new life together. That's what this has been about. Us."

Miles nodded slowly. "And in a week or two, Alex, despondent over his failing business, would be found with a bullet through his head and a gun in his hand, a suicide note left on his computer so no one could dispute the handwriting. One less loose end."

Susan just laughed. "So dramatic, darling. Why go to all that trouble when there's enough for all of us? In a few months, a nice divorce settlement, and as soon as the movie comes out, Lisa and I will too." She smiled at her own small joke and glanced at the other woman to share it. "Alex is no threat to us, he's in this as deep as anyone. So this is what is going to happen." I could see behind her eyes a mind that was busily working, improvising, making it up as she went along. "We're all going to go inside the house, and we're going to wait for another…" She glanced at Lisa. "What time is it?"

Lisa looked at her watch, a thin, diamond tennis-bracelet thing that I was sure had belonged to the real Rachelle. "Ten thirty."

"We're going to wait for another hour and a half," she said, "at which time Rachelle's trust will officially transfer to her. The real Rachelle signed the papers before she left for her anniversary trip—my idea, by the way—so everything is set to go. As soon as Lisa makes a call transferring her assets to an account in the Caymans, you can say whatever you want. In fact, I might even have you on my show and let you tell the world about the fake Rachelle. You can't buy that kind of publicity. Even if the authorities believed you— which they won't— these kinds of investigations take years and years, and the money is already gone."

"Meantime," said Lisa, caressing Susan's shoulder with a brief affectionate smile, "we will be Hollywood's new power couple. I'll be the star I deserve to be and Susan will be the producer she was meant to be, and a little scandal will only add to our cachet. Seriously, you have no idea how many times I've gotten away with playing Rachelle already. Do you really think we would have spent two years planning every little detail of this operation if we didn't think we could pull it off?"

I said, "What about Rick? That was a detail you didn't count on."

Susan said, "He's dead. That's a shame. But no one can link me to his murder. So what if I was there last night? We were old friends from L.A.. There's no reason I shouldn't stop by for a drink. But he seemed agitated and upset, and I left early."